## "He's shooting a

It began to sprinkle in chilly drops. They skittered behind a vehicle and his K-9, Cocoa, looked to him for direction. "Next car, then we dash across the road to the park. Good boy."

He glanced at Sadie, who only nodded, lips quivering. "Now," he murmured, and they bolted onto the empty street. Thunder hollered and another projectile landed two feet ahead of them.

Sadie shrieked and Rocco tightened his grip on her as they sprinted into the pitch-black park. Cocoa kept up with him. He'd been trained for gunfire, so he wasn't skittish of it or the thunder.

Without looking back, Rocco led them toward the woods.

But the killer was on their trail...and time wasn't on their side.

\* \* \*

### *Mountain Country K-9 Unit*

**Jessica R. Patch** lives in the Mid-South, where she pens inspirational contemporary romance and romantic suspense novels. When she's not hunched over her laptop or going on adventurous trips with willing friends in the name of research, you can find her watching way too much Netflix with her family and collecting recipes for amazing dishes she'll probably never cook. To learn more about Jessica, please visit her at jessicarpatch.com.

## Books by Jessica R. Patch

### Love Inspired Suspense

#### Mountain Country K-9 Unit

*Trail of Threats*

#### Texas Crime Scene Cleaners

*Crime Scene Conspiracy*
*Cold Case Target*

#### Quantico Profilers

*Texas Cold Case Threat*
*Cold Case Killer Profile*
*Texas Smoke Screen*

### Love Inspired Trade

*Her Darkest Secret*
*A Cry in the Dark*
*The Garden Girls*

Visit the Author Profile page at LoveInspired.com for more titles.

# Trail of Threats

## JESSICA R. PATCH

**LOVE INSPIRED** SUSPENSE
INSPIRATIONAL ROMANCE

Special thanks and acknowledgment are given to Jessica R. Patch
for her contribution to the Mountain Country K-9 Unit miniseries.

# LOVE INSPIRED® SUSPENSE
## INSPIRATIONAL ROMANCE

Recycling programs
for this product may
not exist in your area.

ISBN-13: 978-1-335-98007-6

Trail of Threats

Copyright © 2024 by Harlequin Enterprises ULC

For questions and comments about the quality of this book, please contact us
at CustomerService@Harlequin.com.

Love Inspired
22 Adelaide St. West, 41st Floor
Toronto, Ontario M5H 4E3, Canada
www.LoveInspired.com

**Printed in U.S.A.**

To appoint unto them that mourn in Zion, to give unto them beauty for ashes, the oil of joy for mourning, the garment of praise for the spirit of heaviness; that they might be called trees of righteousness, the planting of the Lord, that he might be glorified.
—*Isaiah* 61:3

To my Myles. I miss the days of Thomas the Train
and cute bowl haircuts.

# ONE

Someone was watching.

Sadie Owens peered out of her food truck window and scanned Main Street, where she parked her mobile restaurant, Sadie's Subs. She didn't normally stay open this late on weeknights. After five, most businesses closed in Elk Valley, but tonight had been an open house at the elementary school and she'd hoped to catch hungry families who hadn't had time to cook due to the rush from work to the school to meet their children's teachers. She'd done well this evening, even if she'd struggled to manage it alone, but she desperately needed the money and couldn't afford to share tonight's bonus money with another employee. She already struggled to pay her part-time employees—all two of them.

The sun had dipped behind the horizon an hour ago, and now unseen eyes had set their sights on her. The past few days she'd sensed being watched and followed. At first, she'd chalked it up to paranoia. She had reasons to be alert.

Potentially dangerous reasons.

The cream-colored awning with scalloped edges flapped in the cool breeze. Even in August, nights could be cool in Wyoming, but the chill bumps popping along her flesh had nothing to do with the crisp air. She closed the order window and locked it. She'd finished shutting down the grill and putting leftovers away. Her back ached and her feet needed a spa day something fierce but soaking them in Epsom salts would have to do on her tight budget.

She stepped out of the back doors of her truck and locked them, scanning her surroundings. Streetlamps glowed and colorful flowers lined the boutiques and shops along Main Street, but the area was quiet. Elk Valley was a small, tight-knit community of about six thousand residents. Tonight didn't give off safe small-town vibes. Truth be told, Elk Valley wasn't always safe. Ten years ago on Valentine's night, three young men had been lured to a prominent ranch where they'd each taken a bullet to their chests in the barn.

Seth Jenkins, Brad Kingsley and Aaron Anderson had been graduates of Elk Valley High School and members of the local Young Rancher's Club. They hadn't necessarily been nice guys. They'd been bona fide tools and troublemakers—occasionally tangling with the law—but they hadn't deserved to be executed.

Now the Rocky Mountain Killer was back. Three new victims this past Valentine's Day, all former members of the Elk Valley YRC, all shot dead in barns.

Sadie had known them all from around town, despite the fact that the recent victims had moved out of state. She'd even dated Aaron Anderson a few times—she rarely had picked a winner and Aaron had been no exception. She knew that he, along with the other two, had gone through women like water. Love 'em and leave 'em.

Things hadn't ended on amicable terms between her and Aaron. Guess she had no power to change him and his womanizing ways. Her marriage hadn't ended on good terms either. She should have known better than to become involved with Hunter McLeod, but like Aaron, she'd hoped she could coax out the good guy in them. Change them.

Sometimes no good was to be had. And one could never change a person who didn't want to change on their own. She'd had to learn that the agonizing way.

Clouds concealed the moon, only a few stabs of light casting shadows in corners. Clanging behind the nearby alley sent a skitter into her pulse and she clung to her keys and purse as she rounded the truck to the driver's-side door. She had a permit to keep it here overnight, but she liked to have it close by.

In light of two new murders and the cold case looming over Elk Valley, Sadie was on edge, along with the rest of the community.

Footsteps on pavement signaled someone approaching.

She swallowed hard and fumbled with her keys, fingers trembling. The keys fell and she stooped to pick them up. Underneath the pale light shining along the ground, she spotted massive, beat-up tennis shoes on the other side of her truck. Too big to be an average woman's.

"Who's there?" she called, more to let the approaching person know she was aware of him than to garner a response.

Silence.

She struggled to grasp her keys, adrenaline and fear rippling through her. A light cut through the darkness and the footsteps skittered away. In the distance, the figure raced down the alley.

A car approached and parked in front of her truck. Elk Valley's finest. The driver's-side door opened and Officer Rocco Manelli strutted out. If the police cruiser hadn't scared off the creep, Rocco's imposing figure would have. His hair and eyes were as dark as the night and the perpetual scruff around his chin and cheeks added to his menacing effect. If she were a criminal, she would certainly cower at his physicality before even thinking about the fact he had a weapon and was trained to use it.

"Kinda late to be out on a weeknight, isn't it?" he asked in his deep, velvety voice.

"Sorry, *Dad*. I didn't realize I had a curfew," she said, slathering on the sarcasm like butter.

His grin was his best feature, lopsided and mischievous. Other than that, Rocco Manelli was an annoyance. When he worked day shift, he often ate at the food truck. Sadie fed local law enforcement for free. A way to show them they mattered and were appreciated for their service. Rocco always ordered the meatball sub and always spewed unsolicited advice on how to make it better. He was second-generation American Italian, which he assumed gave him a leg up on all Italian dishes.

*A little more basil. A little more gravy—not sauce. Italians call it gravy.* She wasn't Italian. She was a hodgepodge of ethnicities from Irish to English to a small sliver of Native American. She could call it tomato sauce or sauce or whatever she chose. But now was not the time to rile herself up over Officer Manelli's criticism or the fact that he was unbelievably good-looking.

He'd saved her bacon unknowingly.

"Open house at the elementary school tonight. Thought I'd cash in on parents who didn't have time to cook for their families." She blew a heavy breath and relaxed her shoulders. Rocco narrowed his gaze and cocked his head.

"You're spooked. Why?" He closed the distance between them.

Was it that obvious?

No point brushing it off. "It might be nothing." She told him about the man in the ratty tennis shoes. "He ran down the alley between the hardware store and the barber shop when your car approached."

He glanced toward the narrow alley. "Any idea who it might have been?"

She noticed movement in his cruiser and spotted his chocolate Lab, Cocoa. Rocco went nowhere without his trusty K-9 and lately he was needed. July had heated up for Elk Valley and not due to the summer sun. On top of the return of the RMK, a new threat had hit town—an arsonist/murderer. Two already dead right here in Elk Valley.

Elk Valley High's old baseball coach, Ed Towers, who had recently retired.

And Herman Willows, the owner of the feedstore in town. He'd been the first to be killed by fire in his home, then Coach Towers. Rumors and opinions ran rampant—from a new serial killer to the Rocky Mountain Killer changing MO. She didn't believe that.

Officer Manelli was working the arson case with one of the Elk Valley detectives, Jamie Watershed, along with investigating leads to track down the RMK. The guy was burning the candle at both ends. When had Elk Valley become littered with murder and arson? Sadie had a three-year-old son and wanted him to grow up as she had—in a safe small town where people cared about each other.

"I don't have a clue who it was. A man. Not as tall as you but maybe six feet. Lanky. I think he was wearing a hoodie and a ball cap."

"I'll wait on you, see you home."

She wasn't going to turn him down. "I appreciate that. I'll hurry."

"No worries."

"You hungry? I have some leftover roast beef."

"Nah. I ate before shift. You going straight home?" He

searched her eyes in a way that unsettled her—a good one. As if trying to see to her heart and what she truly felt and thought.

"I am. My best friend, Laurie is watching Myles at my house since I knew it would be late when I finished. It's almost his bedtime and I want to be there to read his bedtime story. He's obsessed with Thomas the Train right now. I'm sure Dolly is already at the foot of his bed and ready for it too. I tell you that Irish setter is like a human being. She loves books. I should start a YouTube with her. I can tell her which book to retrieve and she knows it! She'd go viral. Instant sensation."

Rocco grinned. "I'd set up an account just for that."

"I'm tempted." If she liked social media. Unlike her other friends, she steered clear of any kind. She wanted to guard her privacy and Myles's. Not that her ex was online, but he could be and as much as he didn't want to be married, he did at times love to harass her. All she had to do was mention child support and he went crawling back to the rock he scurried out from under or he'd threaten her with attempting to attain custody, which no judge in their right mind would allow, but the fear was real all the same.

She climbed inside the truck and turned the ignition. It sputtered to life. Needed a little engine work done but it would have to wait. Money was stretched thin between the credit cards Hunter had racked up in her name, unbeknownst to her. And the medical bills were as deep as the Grand Canyon. But Myles had been born with neonatal diabetes mellitus. Diagnosed at six months. He needed insulin and Dolly, his medical alert dog, to signal when his blood sugar dropped.

Hunter had wanted no part of that and his threats to take Myles wasn't built on truth, but lies or not, the thought of

Hunter or his coldhearted family having any part in her son's upbringing was unimaginable. They lived fifteen minutes away and had only seen Myles at his birth and once when he turned one. No calls. Nothing but a birthday card with twenty dollars each year and by mail. They'd rather buy a stamp than see their grandson, and Sadie had her suspicions that Hunter had poisoned them about her. Maybe so but how could a grandparent not want to know their grandchild?

She pulled out of her parking spot and headed half a mile down the road to her small house on Elm Circle. She'd grown up in this home and had many fond memories. After Dad had passed last year, it felt empty. She parked in the drive and jumped out, her pulse slowing to normal. Inside, she'd be safe. Her son would greet her with little clammy hands and wet kisses.

Rocco parked behind her and met her at the driver's-side door. "I'll be patrolling. You'll be safe tonight, Sadie. Go in and hug your boy and unwind. You work too hard, though you could try harder with the meatball sub." He winked and her pulse went into a tailspin.

Admiring a handsome man was one thing. Letting it slither into responding to it was a different story. One she had no intention of turning the pages to. She'd stick to Thomas the Train and *Veggie Tales*.

"My meatball sub is my bestseller. I'm keeping it as is." It had been her mother's recipe. The key was extra Parmesan cheese in the meat mixture and no sugar in the marinara.

"Imagine what it could be if you listened to an Italian. I know Italian food." He shrugged.

"Thanks for escorting me home, Officer."

"Rocco. You can call me Rocco."

She walked up her porch steps of the small Craftsman in need of new shutters. She turned back. "I could. I probably won't. Good night." She unlocked the front door, the TV on as background noise and the living room dimly lit. "Laurie, I'm home."

Her best friend since kindergarten exited the hallway. "You're just in time. He's bathed, lathered in that bedtime lotion that makes me want babies and ready for his bedtime story. He asked for you."

She hugged her friend. "Thank you for coming over to watch him. Please let me pay you something."

"You give me free lunch every day which I tell you not to. That's payment enough. Besides, I love the little guy. I'll see myself out and lock the door."

"Thanks, and, Laurie, be careful. Lot of weird things going on these days."

"Don't I know it." She paused. "You be safe too." She hugged her again and let herself out. Sadie went into Myles's room. A small third bedroom with Thomas bedding and light gray walls. His train lamp was lit and he was curled up next to Dolly, running a little blue train over her red furry back.

"Thomas, look out! You'll hit Cranky the Crane!" he said. That boy's imagination was limitless. Dolly was a good sport.

"Hey, pal," she said from the threshold and Myles's big brown eyes lit up.

"Mommy!"

She entered the room and sat on the side of his bed absorbing his tackle as his little arms wrapped around her neck. "You good for Miss Laurie?"

"I was. I missed you."

"I missed you too, baby. Ready for a bedtime story?"

She wished the world was nothing but sweet children's books. But right now, she was afraid she might be in a horror novel. Why had that man come toward her? Who was it? And what did he want?

* * *

The smell of smoke woke Sadie from a fitful sleep. She groggily sat up and inhaled. Had she been dreaming or…no! The smoke was real and had filtered under her door into her bedroom like a deadly fog about to consume her.

Myles!

She raced to the door and tapped the knob. Hot. She used her T-shirt and opened it. Flames licked up the hallway from her room down to Myles's bedroom.

"Mommy!" he called through cries and Dolly barked.

"I'm coming, baby! Hold on." She prayed God would help her rescue her baby boy and lead them safely out of the house. But she couldn't escape her bedroom. She raced to her window, snagging her cell phone from the nightstand on her way. "Siri, call 911," she hollered as she lifted the window and clambered out, then raced around the house to Myles's window. The weather in the evenings had been nice lately and she'd cut the air conditioning and let the breeze filter through the house. Hopefully, she hadn't locked it.

She made it to his window, her heart beating against her ribs. She pushed on the window.

"911. What's your emergency?"

"Fire! My house is on fire and my son is trapped inside. This is Sadie Owens. 2122 Elm Circle."

No! The window was locked. Looking through the pane, smoke filtered under his door and a tongue of fire licked at it.

"Mommy! Mommy!"

"I'm here, baby. Crawl under your covers with Dolly. I'm going to get you out. Stay under the covers, Myles! Be brave for Mommy." She frantically searched for something to break the window and found a ceramic pot of mums. She dumped out the flowers as the dispatcher asked questions, but she ignored her.

She raised the pot and started to swing when something hard clobbered the back of her head. Spots formed before her eyes and the world faded to black.

Rocco Manelli patrolled the quiet streets, letting his mind wander to the pretty owner of Sadie's Subs and her pink food truck with big flowers painted along the side of it. Looked more like a fancy tea cart than a mobile restaurant. But it revealed much about Sadie Owens. She was soft and delicate like the color and flowers of her truck. She was also tough and sassy and smart, which was half the reason he popped in five days a week for lunch when he was on the day shift. He'd switched to the night shift tonight to help an officer who was on vacation. Just one more day and he'd be back to his normal hours and lunches at Sadie's.

While he appreciated her kindness to law enforcement, he never accepted his meals for free. She refused his money, but he made sure to stuff the tip jar with his payment. She was a single mom to a boy who had diabetes. That couldn't be easy. He wasn't sure what the story was on her ex—Rocco had never liked him and he'd been a few years ahead of Rocco in school. But Rocco had gone to school with Sadie, though he was two years older. They hadn't run in the same circle but that didn't mean they hadn't bumped into one another, and they did have one English Lit class together. Sadie had been a big-time reader and sharper than a needle. Last winter he'd had to interview her on the RMK case as she'd dated one of the victims.

This case was driving him nuts and he knew now how his father must've felt all those years ago when he'd been assigned the original case. Dad had spent his entire career trying to find who killed Seth Jenkins, Brad Kingsley and Aaron Anderson. Dad's leads had gone cold and they'd never found the murder weapon, but he'd never stopped investigating. Rocco believed his heart attack a few years ago was due to the stress of that case. And he desperately wanted to solve it and find out who was now, ten years later, killing again. He owed his father. Didn't want his death to be in vain.

The three victims from earlier this year had taken the case nationwide. They'd been killed on their properties across Rocky Mountain states. With notes stabbed into their chests postmortem that read: *They got what they deserved. More to come across the Rockies. And I'm saving the best for last.*

Ominous and terrifying. The RMK had made it clear his mission was not done until he murdered the last on his list. Rocco was grateful he'd been recruited for the task force, comprised of law enforcement from across the Rocky Mountains. It was being led by his old friend and now FBI agent Chase Rawlston.

Dad would be proud that Rocco was on the team task force. A fracture had split through the heart of the community, which was in dire need of healing and restoration. The arson/homicides weren't helping and that new case was leading him down dead ends too.

A plume of smoke rose from the small cove he'd left earlier tonight.

Elm Circle.

Sadie's street.

Earlier she'd almost been approached. His gut clenched and then he heard the dispatcher call for EMT and fire trucks to 2122 Elm Circle. He hit his radio and let dispatch know he was in the area and on his way. He hit the light bar and gunned it down Main Street.

As he approached, a siren's peal alerted him more help was on the way.

"Come on, Cocoa." His chocolate Lab had been with him

for about seven years and was cross-trained in search and rescue as well as arson—accelerant detection. He'd been an asset to the Elk Valley PD lately, and he was family to Rocco. Cocoa bounded out beside him. The house's roof was lit up and the smoke poured like hot breath from a dragon's nose.

He bolted with his K-9 partner toward the house, calling out for Sadie. But no one answered. No time to wait on firefighters. He kicked open the front door, a surge of searing heat blasting him like steam under plastic after being in the microwave too long. "Cocoa, stay."

Smoke filled his lungs and he coughed, covering his nose with his white undershirt, but he entered the house. Dropping to his knees, he crawled through the living room. Whitehot flames ate up the curtains and sides of the walls. Sweat drenched his back, his uniform sticking to his skin. Eyes burning, he called out through a cough.

Crying.

Barking.

Myles and his dog, Dolly. They were trapped. Where was Sadie? She'd never leave her little boy behind. Rocco called out again and reached a narrow hallway but it was engulfed, and he couldn't battle his way through to the bedrooms. He backtracked and ran out the front door, the cool night air a reprieve on his singed skin.

Darting around the house toward the bedroom windows, he spotted a figure lying on the ground.

Sadie!

He barreled toward her, knelt and checked her pulse. Thank God she had one. Her head was bleeding and she was out cold. But she was alive. Cocoa sat, his telltale sign he was alerting to accelerant. No accident but arson.

"Good boy," Rocco said. The dog had smelled the accelerant and if it was the same one here as the other two arsons, it would be turpentine.

A large flowerpot lay beside Sadie. She must have tried to break into Myles's bedroom but someone had stopped her. Why?

Grabbing the pot, he hurled it against the window, breaking it. With his nightstick, he cleaned away the glass and reached inside the window. "Myles, it's Officer Manelli. It's okay, bud."

The boy and his dog were huddled under his Thomas bedcovers and the room was filled with sooty smoke. Rocco climbed inside the room, his eyes stinging and watering. "Hey, Tiger." He grabbed the boy who was crying for his mom and coaxed the Irish setter to come with him, to jump through the window. Then he carefully climbed out with Myles.

EMT were now on the scene and attending to Sadie. One of them approached.

"Hey, Angie," Rocco said, "this is Myles."

"Hi, Myles. I'm Angie. I want to make sure you're okay. Is that all right with you?" she asked the little boy who was shaking in Rocco's arms.

Sadie was loaded onto a backboard and carried to the ambulance. Myles clung to Rocco and the dogs followed.

"I want my mommy. Where's Mommy?" Myles cried.

"She's going to be okay. She's going to the hospital to be checked too. You can see her real soon."

Angie checked Myles's vitals. "Lungs sound clear. Pulse is strong but a doc needs to check him out to be sure."

"I don't want him in the same ambulance as…" He trailed off, not wanting Myles to hear his mother was in an ambulance. It might be too scary and he was already terrified.

"Understood."

"Myles, you get to ride with Miss Angie to the hospital. Okay?"

"I want you." He hugged Rocco's neck in a vise any MMA wrestler would be proud of.

"I'll go with you, okay?" He looked at Angie for approval and she nodded. He could get his patrol car later. Now, only the boy and Sadie mattered.

Rocco hauled Myles into another ambulance, and his medical alert dog and Cocoa jumped inside too.

Was this the work of whoever was killing residents by setting fires to their homes and businesses? Elk Valley had dubbed him the Fire Man. His accelerant was plain old turpentine. Rocco had been working with Elk Valley's one and only homicide detective, Jamie Watershed. As Jamie's investigative chops were needed to focus on Elk Valley, and the Mountain Country K-9 Unit already had three members from town, Jamie hadn't been tapped for the RMK team. Rocco was grateful for the detective's skills on the arson case. They both believed this wasn't the work of a pyromaniac but a killer who used fire as his weapon. Pyros didn't have murder in mind but the thrill of watching things burn.

This guy wanted the victims to die. Sadie must have woken and caught it early or this would have been a completely different story.

They arrived at the hospital and Rocco carried Myles inside, the dogs flanking Rocco as he entered. The next thirty minutes were a blur. Doctors checked Myles and released him but Sadie was still in the ER, so Rocco kept the boy with him, settling him on his lap in a waiting room chair. Myles was soon fast asleep.

Rocco was tired, but he needed to keep going to solve these cases. He'd been out of town so much lately on task force business—first in Idaho, then Montana. He was happy to be on the team but he was also glad to be back in Elk Valley—for now. He might have to travel again and the Elk Valley PD had been more than fair, letting him take off when needed for task force work.

Justice would be served and that meant Rocco's focus was on finding both the Fire Man and the Rocky Mountain Killer.

The RMK case had been reopened with the deaths of Peter Windham and Henry Mulder. Peter was a good Christian guy living in Denver and had never wronged Naomi Carr-Cavanaugh, who the task force believed had been the catalyst to the murders. She'd been invited to the dance at the Young Rancher's Club by Trevor Gage but apparently under false pretenses. According to witnesses, Trevor and his friends had been playing a big joke to humiliate her, although Trevor still stuck to his claim that he liked Naomi, that it wasn't a joke, but his friends believed the opposite and it had gotten way out of hand.

Peter had been Naomi's friend. So why would the RMK kill him?

In Montana, Henry Mulder—who had been a brawler and troublemaker—had been shot too.

In Sagebrush, another victim had taken a 9mm to the chest. Luke Randall. He'd been a Young Rancher's Club member and a troublemaker like Henry and the first three victims. Unfortunately, by the time the task force made it to his house to warn him that he was likely a target, he was dead in the barn.

The consensus among the team was that the RMK's threat about saving the best for last referred to Trevor Gage himself—punishment for the alleged prank on Naomi Carr-Cavanaugh, who had been cleared of the murders. However, her brother, Evan Carr was still on their radar. As was Ryan York, whose sister, Shelly, had died by suicide after dating one of the victims, Seth Jenkins. That gave Ryan motive to kill one of the victims, but what about the rest?

As of right now, neither Ryan or Evan could be found for new interviews.

The ER doctor returned to the waiting room.

"Can we see her, Doc?" he asked.

The doctor nodded. "She's going to be fine. A slight concussion. She got knocked on the head good. We want to monitor her a few hours and then she'll be ready to go, Officer."

Rocco's blood boiled. He would find this guy. At the moment, he couldn't be sure if it was the work of the Fire Man or someone else using fires to come after Sadie. Either way, he wasn't going to let the culprit go free.

With Myles in his arms, Rocco used a hand to open the curtain. Sadie lay on the hospital bed with her eyes closed. Soot and dirt covered her face mixed with a few white lines from tears washing down her cheeks. No doubt over her son. Quietly, he entered, Myles asleep on his shoulder, his warm face buried in the side of Rocco's neck and a little blue train in his tiny grip. The sleeping child in his arms, relying on him and feeling safe in his presence, shifted something loose in his chest and he ran his hand over the boy's dark cap of hair, sweaty and curled around his ears. Not that he'd never thought about settling down and having children—his job had to come first.

More than anything he needed to solve this case, and find the Rocky Mountain Killer. To finish what his father had started and to bring this town back together.

His phone buzzed in his pocket and he finagled it into his hand and checked. While the doctor had been examining Myles, Rocco had texted the task force's tech analyst, Isla Jimenez, who also worked for the EVPD, for any information on Sadie he didn't already know having grown up in the same town as her. He'd also texted the task force leader, Chase Rawlston. He had three texts.

Isla had no more information than he already had and was working on finding Sadie's ex. Last known address was in Cheyenne.

Chase had texted about a team meeting at headquarters tomorrow but otherwise to do what he needed to in order to see this case through. He texted back he'd be at the meeting and 10-4 on following the case through. He wanted to see it through. Wanted to make sure Sadie and her son were safe—that all of Elk Valley was safe from this arsonist and murderer.

If he could make a single connection between the victims it might help leave a breadcrumb trail to his perp. He texted Isla and asked if she wouldn't mind searching any connections between the victims and Sadie. She quickly responded she was on it.

The last text was from the fire chief letting him know what he already suspected. The fire was deliberately set and turpentine was used as an accelerant.

Between this case and working the Rocky Mountain murders, he might be in a heart-health issue like his own father. The stress was immeasurable and the frustration mounting. But like Grandfather always said, "Cast all your cares onto God because He cares for you." Rocco was working to do that very thing but it felt like the only shoulders bearing the burden right now were his own.

It wasn't true.

Deep within he knew that, but it felt that way. Felt like God wasn't moving in the situation at all. As if He'd abandoned not only Elk Valley but Rocco—and Rocco's father before him. Why couldn't they catch a break? Why did more people have to perish? Seemed unfair.

He reminded himself they lived in a broken world with broken people who had freewill choice and many of those choices were evil.

Sadie's eyes fluttered open and she blinked a few times, then touched her sore head. When she saw Rocco and Myles she scooted up, drawing her light sheet up around her chest. "Is he okay?" she whispered, noticing he was asleep.

"Shaken up. I've been with him the whole time."

"How did he get out?" She covered her mouth with her hands, eyes wide. "I was trying to break his window when someone hit me on the head. I was so scared."

Rocco wanted to go to the bed, to hold her hand, but Myles was still asleep and he didn't want to wake him, didn't want him to hear the scary, grown-up talk about to happen. He had to question Sadie. "I was patrolling. Got the call and made it to the scene first. I saw what you'd tried to do and finished it for you. Myles and Dolly are fine." Both dogs lay at his feet, Cocoa's head resting on his foot.

"Thank you. I'm not sure I know how to repay you."

"You could always add that extra basil to the meatball sub," he teased, hoping to lighten the tension.

It worked.

Sadie smiled. "Nice try."

"I need to ask you a few questions," he said softly, so as to not wake the child. "Before he gets up."

"Of course."

"Tell me what happened tonight once you came home."

Sadie walked him through the moment she entered the house, to when she was bashed on the head. "I don't understand why someone would target me or want to hurt my son."

"Do you have any enemies?"

She shook her head and winced, touching the bump. "No. Well…not any that would want to kill me and Myles. Jack

Norwood is my biggest competitor and consistently asks to buy me out, but I don't think he'd try to kill me. And he wouldn't have any reason to also want to kill the others who've died in the recent arsons—that I know about. I assume you believe it's connected."

Sadie was sharp and her green eyes drilled into his, her long blond hair a little disheveled. She was striking. He couldn't deny that. "The accelerant is the same as the other two victims. I'll go by your place and check it out myself but I got a text from the fire chief, confirming. Anyone else you'd consider a rival or enemy?"

Shifting on the bed, Sadie forced herself upright and sipped on a foam cup of water. "My ex-husband. Hunter McLeod—I took my maiden name back after the divorce. He left when Myles was diagnosed. Couldn't handle it but I think it was an out for him. One he'd been wanting for a while. Sometimes he calls and gives me a hard time, but he didn't have anything against Coach Towers—he played high school baseball for him and loved him. Nor did he have issues with Mr. Willows from the feedstore. At least not that I knew about. But I don't think he'd go so far as to kill us either."

What a complete waste of space. Rocco would never shirk his responsibilities or leave someone in the lurch. Sadie was a brave and tough woman, full-time mom and business owner, plus she often volunteered at the community food bank and soup kitchen. In his eyes, Sadie Owens was a true hero.

"I'm sorry about that," he said.

She placed the cup of water on the side table. "Myles is sleeping so deeply."

"Adrenaline crash is exhausting."

"I'm pretty tired too." Her face paled. "I have no idea where we're going to stay now. Do you know if my home is salvageable?"

Rocco couldn't say, but from what he'd seen he would guess no. He hated being the bearer of bad news. Sadie didn't seem to have much good news in her life. "I don't know for certain."

"Do you think this guy will try again when he figures out we're not dead?"

That was an excellent question and one he hated to answer, because once again it wouldn't be good news.

# TWO

Jamie had dropped Rocco back at his cruiser that he'd left at Sadie's, and now Rocco sat in the vehicle and stared at the house. Nothing but charred remains. Anything inside would be smoke-infested and ruined. Sadie did not deserve this. None of the victims had. But she was the only one to survive, which meant they might have a leg up in the investigation. He opened the door and waited for Cocoa to bound out with him. About thirty minutes ago, Sadie's friend and babysitter, Laurie, had swung by the hospital to sit with Myles until Sadie was cleared to leave, and a uniformed officer had also been stationed at her room, just in case. Laurie had offered Sadie a place to stay and Rocco had remained silent.

If this guy returned, it could put Laurie in danger and she could lose her house too—or worse. Rocco had no profile on this suspect other than he wasn't an arsonist but a killer using fire as his choice of weapon. That meant he wasn't a hands-on killer, indicating he could possibly be physically weak or lacking in his confidence. Fire was power he didn't have on his own. But why had he targeted these particular victims? That was what stuck in Rocco's craw.

He rubbed his buddy's head and knelt. "Alert!"

Cocoa sniffed the air and bolted across Sadie's yard, Rocco on his heels. Cocoa returned to the same place he'd alerted previously—to the point of origin. The back of the house nearest the bedrooms. It would have eaten the wall then charged down the hallway, trapping Sadie and her son in their bedrooms. Unlike Coach Towers and Herman Willows, Sadie had awoken and smelled the smoke, giving herself the chance to escape before the entire house went up in flames.

His phone rang and he glanced at the screen and grinned. His MCTF colleague, US Marshal Meadow Ames.

He answered. "Hey, M."

"Heard there was another fire in Elk Valley. Chase texted. Thought I'd call and see what's what."

"I don't know much." He explained everything he did know and Sadie and Myles's condition.

"Wow. That's rough. If I can help with anything let me know. I owe you for all you did to help me and Ian."

Last month he'd aided Meadow and her former witness Ian Carpenter, whose cover in WITSEC had been blown. They'd all nearly died. Now Ian was on the MCK-9 team with his German shepherd, Lola. And he and Meadow were an item.

"We ain't keeping score. You know that."

"Good. I don't really want to come to Elk Valley anyway," she teased and laughed. He pictured her green eyes lighting up as she hooted. Meadow was like a sister to him. Knowing she had Ian in her life now was super cool. A pang of loneliness hit him in the ribs. It had been awhile since he'd dated anyone. Work always came first and that wasn't fair to a woman. Mom had been good about Dad's up-and-leaving in the middle of supper or in the night. Being a cop's wife was a job of its own and could take a toll.

"Good. I don't want you to," he jested. "I'm stressed out, not gonna lie, but we'll figure it out. How are you feeling about our possible suspects?"

"Ryan York and Evan Carr?"

"No, the other suspects we don't have," he teased sarcastically.

She snorted. "A tall blond guy wearing sunglasses and a ski cap isn't a lot to go on."

"True. But he's been seen with our labradoodle. If he hangs on to her, we might catch another lead." MCK-9 rookie Ashley Hanson had wanted a compassion K-9 for the team to help victims' families, but it wasn't in the budget so her fancy-pants father had donated the labradoodle to the task force. Liana Lightfoot, their K-9 trainer, had been working with her but Cowgirl, who had a distinct dark splotch on her right ear, had been stolen by the Rocky Mountain Killer. She hadn't had her tags but she had been chipped and the information had been given to the PD. Posters had been put up and tech analyst Isla had done a social media blast to help find her. Sure enough, tips had come in.

She'd been spotted in Idaho, where the last victim was murdered. A witness had seen her with a tall blond man wearing sunglasses and a ski cap. Then their team leader, Chase Rawlston, had received a text from the man they suspected was the RMK, taunting him that he had Cowgirl. He'd sent a photo through a burner phone of the labradoodle on a dog bed with a blanket and toys. He said he'd renamed her Killer, and she wore a pink collar with her new name spelled out in rhinestones. More recently, Chase had received another taunt that the labradoodle was pregnant.

At least the picture suggested he was taking care of her.

"We can only hope so," Meadow said. "Maybe someone will see her with him. I don't know. It feels impossible at the moment but God is in the business of making the impossible possible, so we keep praying and trusting."

"Amen," he said.

"Keep me posted and watch your back," Meadow said.

"Will do." He ended the call and he and Cocoa trudged back to the cruiser. It hadn't been quite an hour. Sadie would still be at the hospital. Once he turned into the parking lot in the ED, he found a parking space near the trees by the road. The lot was packed for this time of night. He strode across the asphalt, and his skin prickled. He paused, Cocoa hesitating with him, and listened, looked. Rocco didn't see anyone but his gut wasn't usually wrong and it was warning him that danger lurked.

Inside, he found Sadie standing at the edge of her bed and Myles sitting on it. Her friend Laurie smiled. She was pretty in a girl-next-door kind of way and a few inches shorter than Sadie, who was about five-five if he had to guess.

"What brings you back, Officer?" Sadie asked. "Did you go by my house?"

"I did. I wish I had better news."

Tears filled her eyes. "I grew up in that house. All my memories of my family, my father. Photos."

"Officer Rocco," Myles said through a yawn and reached for him. "Hold me." The kid was probably exhausted. Rocco definitely was. Rocco opened his arms and scooped up the little boy.

"Hey, Tiger. How you doing?"

"I'm sleepy." He yawned again and Dolly nuzzled next to Rocco's legs to be near her person.

"Me too." He looked at Sadie. "I know you plan to stay with Laurie, but I'd like to offer you another option. A little out of bounds concerning protocol, but I can't be sure this guy won't..." He let it hang, not wanting to scare little Myles. "I don't want to put anyone else in danger. You and Myles are welcome to come and stay with me. Cocoa can track accelerant a quarter of a mile away. No one is going to get the jump on you. You'll be safer there."

"I don't know," she said hesitantly, her bottom lip tucking between her teeth.

"I want to stay with you," Myles said to Rocco. "You're my hero. Like Thomas the Train."

Rocco's insides turned to complete goo. He didn't feel like a hero. He was working two cases with no leads and people kept dying. Nothing heroic about not being able to save innocent lives.

"Can we stay with Officer Rocco, Mommy? Please," he begged. Rocco avoided making eye contact with Sadie. The little guy was putting her on the spot, but Rocco wasn't going to reprimand him for it. His small ranch truly was the safest and he had two spare rooms, a big, fenced-in backyard for the dogs and Myles to play and the mountains as a backdrop. He even had two horses in his own pasture. Myles might enjoy riding a horse.

Sadie blew out her cheeks in a long sigh and then smiled. "Are you sure we're not an imposition?"

"Not at all. I'm out a little ways, but not too far that you can't drive into work in about fifteen to twenty minutes."

Sadie worked her bottom lip with her teeth. "I don't want to put anyone in danger." She looked at Laurie.

"I'm not afraid, Sadie, but I agree that with Rocco's dog you would be safer. Still, I want to keep Myles while you work."

"Are you sure?" Sadie asked her.

"Positive. Let me handle getting you some clothing and toiletries together and I'll take care of Myles too. I already put a text out to the church ladies. You'll be taken care of. Guaranteed."

Sadie's eyes filled with moisture. "Thank you." She nodded at Rocco. "I guess we can, for a few days max. Surely you'll catch this guy by then."

Rocco hoped so, but even the best detectives didn't always solve the crime. His dad had been proof of that.

Sadie hugged Myles as he left with Laurie with the promise of ice cream and new trains. She had no clue what she'd do without her friendship and the rallying of her church family. Already she had received dozens of texts letting her know she was in their prayers and anything she might need, to let them know.

Sadie's biggest reservation about staying with Rocco Manelli was she didn't want rumors circulating that she was living with a man—even though she was not. Rocco might grate her nerves when it came to sandwiches, but he had a stellar reputation and was known as an honorable, upstanding man of faith, full of integrity. Sadie had never seen him any other way, sans his criticism of her food. But he was jovial about that too. No one would think it was untoward, especially since his dog was trained in accelerant detection.

Myles clearly felt safe with him. If he hadn't driven by, hadn't paid attention to the smoke this story might have ended differently. Sadie could not imagine a life without her sweet baby boy in it. He was pure joy even on the hard days and they'd had many hard days. At the moment, her stomach was in a myriad of knots. She now had to find a place to live, and the costs she was about to incur wouldn't break the bank because she was already basically broke. She had a business to run or she wouldn't make an income. Besides, Myles needed insulin, which wasn't cheap, and neither was insurance. Most of her paycheck went to that and she was thankful for medicine that kept her son alive. She'd never complain or regret paying the steep costs to keep him well.

But it was a factor.

Hunter hadn't paid a dime in child support and the one

time she mentioned taking him to court, bad things had happened.

He'd slashed all her tires on the food truck. Not that she could prove it, and she hadn't gone to the police for fear he'd turn it around and threaten to take Myles. Her dad had insisted there was no way he could and they were empty threats. But it wasn't worth the risk.

Surely, Hunter wouldn't have set fire to kill them in order to keep from paying child support in the future. That would be cruel even for him.

"I should tell you something," she said. "I'm almost positive Hunter…slashed my food truck tires once." She told him about the events leading up to the incident. "But I don't think he'd try to harm our persons. He's not a killer. Just a hothead." Who could be dangerous. He'd gotten into a bar fight when they'd been in Jackson Hole on their honeymoon. He'd never hurt Sadie, but when he was angry…it could be scary.

Rocco frowned and folded his arms over his wide chest as Cocoa sat patiently beside him. "I don't want to rule him out. If he's desperate for money and thinks you might take him to court…anything is possible. I'll do a check and see where he's been of late." He jotted the information on his notepad.

The doctor entered and cleared her to leave with promises to rest and not overdo it. She was a single mom and the breadwinner of their little family. Rest was not a viable option for her. Every day she prayed God would supply her needs and provide for her and Myles. Her house burning to ash didn't feel like provision but removal. Where would she live? She didn't have a house payment because Dad had paid it off a few years ago. Rent. Mortgage. Sadie couldn't afford either of those things.

"You look concerned. I know you don't know me well, but I promise nothing sketchy will happen with me—"

"I'm not worried about you hitting on me, Officer Manelli." Sadie waved him off with a smirk. "You've had millions of chances by now. Besides, I don't have time for romantic relationships. Myles is my number one priority, and I'm too busy between parenting and work for anything extra." Especially now that she was trying to add a catering business to her list of jobs. She needed the extra income and she enjoyed cooking and serving others. Seeing people come together through food made her world go round. "I can't even make it to Wednesday morning Bible study or the monthly women's book club, which would be amazing."

"I do remember you loving to read. You were in my English Lit class when you were just a freshman."

"Well, I never said I wasn't smart." She grinned. "But my point is a man is the last of my worries. It's… I have a lot of financial responsibilities and now I'm homeless."

Homeless.

Her lungs squeezed and her heart sprinted. She bent over her knees and took three cleansing breaths. God had this. Didn't He? Because if He didn't, no one did.

"Hey, it's going to be okay. I know it sounds trite but it will be." Rocco's hand rested on her shoulder, strong and warm and reassuring.

It did sound trite but he meant well. "I know," she whispered but she wasn't sure she believed it. Seemed like the right thing to say, though. Dad would have known what to do. He'd been her champion since birth, and whether she was riding a bike, cheerleading or owning her own business he'd always spurred her on her journey with encouragement and sound advice. She missed him now more than ever. She needed strong arms to run into, to shield her and make her feel safe.

She knew she had the church and community friends to

help but she still felt utterly helpless and alone. And a murderer was out there and possibly not done with her yet.

"Come on, let me take you to the house where you can clean up and sleep a few hours. You need it."

Sadie didn't have much time to rest. It was nearing 4:00 a.m. and she had prep work for today. She prided her business on using fresh ingredients daily. Fresh and never frozen meant a lot of prepping vegetables and simmering sauces for the sandwiches. She made the bread daily and ensured the leftover bread went to the soup kitchen in town.

"I need to be at the food truck by six. Lunch begins at eleven and I have a lot to do."

Rocco didn't offer her any solutions like taking the day off or using old bread, which she was thankful for. "It's a public place and close to the station. So I'm not going to say what I'm thinking."

"That I shouldn't be there at all?"

"You were attacked. I'm concerned." But he escorted her from the hospital room and to the parking lot, Cocoa obediently heeling at Rocco's feet. Dawn wouldn't break for another hour and a half and the air had a nip to it. But she didn't mind. The cool air was a reprieve to her fevered skin and nausea. The doctor had called her in something for it and prescription-strength pain reliever for when the medicines they'd given her at the hospital wore off.

She was going to have a doozy of a headache. Sadly, she had no time to be sick. Life wouldn't wait on her.

"I can help you prep for today's meals. I know my way around a kitchen."

"So you have said dozens of times," she teased. It felt nice to lighten the mood. Everything else in her life was heavier than she could carry.

He laughed. Rich and infectious. The kind that reached his

ebony eyes and created a joyful sparkle. When was the last time she'd seen a sparkle in her eyes? Always when Myles made her laugh. He was her sweet bundle of joy and happiness.

"Don't you need to sleep?" she asked.

"I think I have time to help you knead bread and sauté vegetables for the lunch crowd. I actually love to cook. It's therapy for me."

"Me too."

"Ah, we have something in common."

"Besides a killer who wants to turn me to ash. I'm not a phoenix. I get burned, I'm not rising up."

"I'd say you already are, Sadie. Your house was burned to rubble and here you are talking about making food for the community. You're not being held back even though you're afraid. That's bravery at its finest in my eyes." He nudged her shoulder playfully but she caught the seriousness in his tone. His words soothed like healing balm to her sore heart.

"I don't feel brave, Officer."

"I'm not sure any brave person feels brave when acting courageously. Bravery means moving forward in spite of the fear. Not running from it but tackling it head-on. That's precisely what you're doing. No matter why you're doing it—though I imagine for your son—you're doing it. And I want to help you."

He already had. A fresh wave of strength coursed through her and for the first time all night, she didn't feel quite as alone.

"I appreciate the offer and as long as you steer clear of my marinara for the meatball subs, and the meatballs altogether, I'll allow it." She held in a grin and he laughed again.

"I can't make promises like that, Sadie. When I see a

remedy to make food better, I have to apply it. And I could make your sandwiches sing."

"Yeah, well, I'm fine with a low hum."

He laughed even louder now. Maybe the day would be okay.

A crack echoed on the air.

"Gunfire!" Rocco bellowed and shoved Sadie to the ground.

# THREE

Gunfire erupted and bullets sprayed the parked cars closest to Rocco's cruiser. His heart thrummed wildly as he shielded Sadie from the barrage of projectile. Cocoa looked to Rocco for instruction. "Stay down," he murmured, "the both of you." Rocco raised his head up, keeping to the trunk of a car for safety. The shooter had blended into the night, nothing but shadows and stillness.

Rocco gripped his gun, weighing if he should fire back. The cover of night not only concealed the gunman but any other civilians who might be out here. At a hospital, the time wouldn't matter. Deciding on caution, he didn't return fire. But they weren't going to be able to stay down all night.

His cruiser was parked two cars over, and the shooter might be waiting for them to race to it for cover. The hospital was about fifty feet away. Neither option was decent. Across the street was a park with towering trees, benches and play equipment. Beyond the wooded area was Main Street, with shops, alleys and the Elk Valley PD.

The park was their best option. "We need to cut through the park to Main Street. We can use these cars as cover until we make it to the road then rush across. Use the trees and equipment to hide us then through the woods to Main Street.

You up for a run and a hike?" He knew Cocoa would stick by his side.

"I'm not up for dying in a hospital parking lot, which is ironic and sad. So, yeah. Yeah, I'm up for it," Sadie said through shallow breaths, her hands shaking but her voice steady.

Instead of moving toward the cruiser, where the sniper might be focusing his trained gun, he led Sadie in the opposite direction, as if doubling back to the ER. If the shooter pulled the trigger again, it would bring attention. Rocco was surprised no one had called it in. Surely, hospital staff and patients had heard two rounds being fired. But he didn't hear sirens and he didn't want to hit the radio and give away their position. A rumble of thunder rolled overhead and lightning flashed across the sky.

They may have passed it off as the storm was rolling in. The lightning wasn't working to their advantage. Pops of light might reveal them. But it might also expose the person trying to kill them. Grabbing Sadie's hand, he stayed crouched low, moving around cars and keeping below their windows for cover. He paused at each car, listening for footsteps to determine if the gunman was closing the distance between them, figuring out their position and readying himself.

Another boom thundered as a bullet slammed into the car they'd hid behind before making it to this one. Another bullet fired at the next thunderous roar and hit a car an aisle over.

"He's shooting at random. Trying to flush us out," Rocco whispered. "He doesn't know our position." It began to sprinkle in chilly drops. "Let's go." They skittered to the next vehicle, a gray Toyota Tundra. Ducking behind the tailgate, Rocco waited as the sprinkle turned to a soft but steady rain. Cocoa looked to him for direction. "Next car, then we dash across the road to the park. It's okay, boy. Good boy."

Sadie only nodded, her lips quivering and raindrops dotting her lashes. He gripped her wet, slippery hands and they rushed to the next car. "Now," he murmured and they darted over a patch of grass outlined in concrete curbs, a few trees lining the stretch of lawn, and bolted over it and onto the empty, open street.

As they dashed across, thunder hollered and another projectile landed on a street lamp two feet ahead of them.

They'd been made.

Rocco had anticipated but hoped it wouldn't happen.

Sadie shrieked and Rocco tightened his grip on her, hauling her across the wet pavement. She stumbled, unable to keep up with his gait but righted herself and they sprinted into the pitch-black park dense with trees. Cocoa kept up with him. He'd been trained for gunfire, so he wasn't skittish of it or the thunder.

Without looking back or pausing, Rocco led Sadie across the middle of the park, weaving through playground equipment and toward the woods.

But the killer was on their trail.

Time wasn't on their side.

Light, steady rain grew heavier but that might work to their benefit, blurring the vision of their gunman. A bullet pinged the metal merry-go-round and they ducked, taking cover behind a small wooden snow cone stand. They had about sixty feet to the woods. No one would be in the park. No one was calling it in. Now that he was out of earshot, he hurried and radioed backup, giving their location and noting the shooter was armed and dangerous.

Sirens could now be heard beyond the woods onto Main Street, which meant the killer would hear them too. "I think we should stand firm here. The police will either scare him away or show up and catch him. If we run for the woods, he might get one last shot off and it could be fatal."

With their backs to the side of the building, they waited. Sadie let out a shaky breath. "I guess it's safe to assume the killer who tried to burn me and my son alive is the same person shooting at us now. You said he wasn't a pyromaniac obsessed with fire but a killer who uses fire for a weapon. Guess he's got a second-choice weapon."

Rocco peeked behind the snow cone stand, seeing nothing. The sirens pealed louder as they approached. "He's improvising. He can't burn down everything you walk inside. He has no choice but to adapt."

"Great. A flexible killer."

Rocco couldn't mask a smirk. He appreciated Sadie's snark even in scary times. He recognized it for what it was—a coping mechanism.

Light flashed and cars lined the road behind them and the hospital parking lot. "Let's wait a few minutes before coming out of the park. Make sure they find him or clear the area. Better safe than—"

"Dead," she supplied.

"I was going to say sorry, but yeah. Dead fits."

"Manelli!" a voice called and Rocco recognized it. The detective he was working with on the arsons/homicides cases. "It's me, Jamie!" he called. "Parking lot is cleared. The shooter was either on foot or made his way inside the hospital to hide. PD is inside hunting him down but I think he got away on foot. Maybe parked nearby. Cruisers are canvassing the area for several blocks."

Rocco led Sadie and Cocoa out from behind the snow cone stand. "He couldn't have gotten far. Not this time of night—or morning should I say."

Jamie approached. He had Sioux heritage and had moved

here five years ago from Billings, Montana, where he'd worked homicide. He was tall and lean and full of grit, with gray streaking his jet-black hair. There were a few crinkles on his bronzed face, lining the outer corners of his dark eyes, and he had a long, narrow nose.

"My car's parked on the edge of the street. Let me get you both somewhere safer. We can talk in the confines of the car. I'd feel better." He motioned them to follow, his gun in his right hand.

They followed him through the park to the unmarked charger at the curb. Rocco opened the back passenger door for Sadie and Cocoa, then climbed into the front passenger side. Jamie buckled up and they headed down the street. "What can you tell me?" he asked Rocco. "You see him? He say anything?" The windshield wipers squeaked as they rotated across the glass. He noticed Sadie shiver and switched on the heat, pointing a vent toward the back of the car.

"No, he didn't say anything. He used the thunder as cover to shoot. He didn't even wait a full night to retaliate. What do you make of that?" Rocco asked.

Jamie glanced through the rearview mirror. "Are you sure you don't have any enemies, Miss Owens? This feels like someone who finds it urgent to harm you. Do you have any unsavory information on someone? A reason why someone wants you immediately dead?"

Sadie winced. "My husband can be a little vindictive and ugly, but it's hard to think he might want us dead. And I can't think of anyone—not even Jack Norwood who wants to buy me out—who would hate me so much they'd do this kind of fiery vengeance."

"Our fire guy didn't randomly choose his victims. He had reasons—possibly warped reasoning, but they were targeted.

I wish we had a connection. You're our only survivor." Jamie sighed. "I don't mean to frighten you."

"Too late," she said.

After a few more questions, Detective Watershed circled the block and returned them to the hospital parking lot where Elk Valley PD were still stationed.

"You need anything, Roc?" the detective asked.

"No. Do send some extra patrol around Laurie Bennett's house. She has Myles for the night. While we believe Sadie is the intended target, we can't rule out the boy."

Sadie's heart lurched into her throat, dizzying her. Why would anyone want to hurt an innocent child?

Child support?

Her cell phone rang—the only thing at the moment she had that actually belonged to her. It was Laurie. "Hey, Laurie, everything okay?"

"Yes and no. I have a go bag for you and Myles is agitated, crying for you and Officer Rocco. He's scared. I hoped being here in a safe and familiar place would settle him, but it hasn't. I'm sorry."

"No, it was my mistake for even allowing it. He's been traumatized." They both had. "I'll come by now, and thank you. For everything."

"What's going on?" Rocco's dark eyes flashed with worry.

"Myles wants me." She left out that he'd also asked for the officer. She hoped the attachment wouldn't last long. Rocco had saved him from fire, which made him a hero and Myles was all about superheroes. Not to mention he needed male attention in his life—even if he didn't realize it—and Rocco, the rescuer, fit the bill. But Rocco wasn't his father or anyone who wanted to be saddled with a kid's expectations. The man had a full plate, and being a babysitter or crutch for a preschooler wasn't it. "Can we swing by Laurie's and pick him up?"

"Absolutely. We'll go now."

Rocco, Cocoa and Sadie clambered out of the car and Sadie thanked the detective for the ride and the extra patrols around Laurie's. Once they were inside Rocco's cruiser, Sadie leaned her head against the headrest. The pain meds were wearing off and a dull thump had begun behind her right eye. She was worn slap out but her mind was keyed up. She'd made a mistake letting Laurie take Myles for the night. She'd wanted to protect him and had been unsure how long it would take for formal statements and interviews. Myles didn't need to hear it.

And truth be told, she needed him right now too.

"We're going to do everything in our power to get this guy," Rocco said.

"I hope so. Will you be at the house all night or do you have to go back to your night shift."

"I texted with the captain and he's put another officer on the shift. I return to the day shift Monday. I can be with you during the nights then."

"Why do criminals always creep out after dark?" she muttered. She already knew the answer. The wicked felt safe at night under an inky sky to slink and slither around doing harm and plotting evil. They loved to lurk in the shadows.

Once at Laurie's, Sadie unbuckled. "I'll be right back." She hustled up the wooden porch steps and Laurie opened the door before she knocked. "Is he okay?"

"He's asleep now but it's fitful and I fear if he wakes and doesn't have you, he'll freak out." Laurie's eyes were tired but her smile was sympathetic. "Come on in. I have bags for the both of you."

Inside, two large duffel bags and Myles's car seat were on

the end of the couch where Myles was sleeping. Dolly lay below, her head resting on the couch near his face. She loved that boy almost as much as Sadie. "Thank you. I couldn't ask for a better friend." She hugged her, feeling tears sting the back of her eyes.

"We're more than friends, silly. We're sisters of the heart."

"Sister from another mister," Sadie teased and Laurie laughed.

Sadie scooped up Myles, shushing him as he whimpered in his sleep. "It's okay, Mommy has you." Dolly followed as Laurie carried the bags to Rocco's cruiser. He bounded out and took the bags and car seat from Laurie, placing them in the back seat.

Sadie secured Myles in his car seat, the tuckered out little guy not even waking, only shifting and whimpering again. Once he was buckled in, Dolly jumped inside with him and Cocoa.

They waited for Laurie to enter the house and lock the door. Once Rocco seemed sure that she was safe, he pulled onto the street. "She seems great," he whispered.

She nodded and felt a teensy prickle of jealousy. Laurie was sweet and beautiful and loved Jesus. But the idea of Rocco expressing interest made her chest tighten. A stupid reaction. Laurie was a catch. She only needed the right man in her life, and Rocco was a good guy.

But still.

"She's the best. I don't know what I'd do without her." That was solid truth.

"What's her story?" he asked quietly.

"Why? You interested?" she asked, hoping to conceal the fact she didn't love the idea. She had no reason not to love it.

"Curious," he said and cast her a glance. "I'm curious about everything. Maybe that's what makes me a decent cop."

She grinned. "We've been friends since kindergarten. I would make pretend food in a play kitchen and she would eat it. She hates cooking. We pretty much do everything together. She warned me about Hunter when I was going to culinary school. I should've listened to her but I didn't."

"Sometimes we have to learn it by experience, not words. Never goes down easy, though."

"Amen."

He smirked. "What's her favorite sandwich?"

"The meatball sub."

Rocco lightly laughed, so as to not wake Myles. "That is a good friend. To lie right to your face."

"Ha ha." She held in her own laughter at his jesting.

Once they turned off the main road it was nothing but pastureland and mountains in the distance. Wyoming was a beautiful state and she'd never even dreamed of moving elsewhere. Fresh air, beautiful scenery and kind people.

Rocco pulled onto a road with wire fencing. Up ahead a cozy light shone from inside a small ranch. "Home sweet home," he said as he turned down the long gravel drive.

He parked outside the house and then he and Cocoa bounded out. Sadie took Myles from his car seat, carrying the sleeping boy in her arms while Dolly heeled at her side. Rocco unlocked the front door and she stepped inside the foyer that opened up to the living room.

"I'll grab your bags." He pointed to the hallway to the right. "My guest room is the second door on the left. Queen bed, so it should be comfy for you both."

"It'll be perfect. Thank you."

Rocco darted outside and she surveyed his masculine home done in earth tones and pops of red from the blanket on the back of his leather couch to a huge painting of poppies hanging above the mantel on the fireplace. She wasn't sure what to expect from Rocco Manelli's house but it wasn't what she'd consider a bachelor pad. Tasteful art and nice furniture on old hardwood flooring. She smelled a hint of vanilla that overrode the heavy garlic scent from an earlier meal. Rocco's home was cozy and she instantly relaxed.

He returned with her bags and she followed him to the guest room.

After he gave her a quick tour and showed her where she could find clean towels and extra blankets, she laid Myles in the comfy bed with the thick red comforter—clearly Rocco loved red—and tiptoed back into the living room.

Rocco was in a state-of-the-art kitchen with a pot simmering on the stove. "I know I need to go to bed but I'm not tired. Thought I'd make some hot chocolate."

"If I go to sleep now, I'll never wake up in time to prep for today." She studied his double oven and gas stove. Expensive cookware and marble countertops. She only dreamed of a kitchen this amazing.

"You want a cup?"

"Sounds good."

When the milk was warm he added a cocoa mix and stirred it then poured them each a steaming cup and brought them to the kitchen table in the breakfast nook. "My grandma, Luna, always said hot chocolate cures all hurts. I believed that until Katie Quigmire dumped me my sophomore year. Chocolate did not heal my wounded teenage heart."

Sadie grinned as she sipped her drink. She liked Rocco. A lot. And that was a whole other kind of fire but equally as dangerous.

After hot chocolate, in mostly comfortable silence, Rocco talked Sadie into getting at least three hours of shut-eye before she had to be up to work on bread for the lunch and supper crowds. With him helping, she wouldn't have to start so early. He had no idea what her financial situation was but if he had to guess, being a single mom with a child who had medical needs couldn't be easy.

He must have dozed on the couch because movement startled him awake and Cocoa raised himself up from the floor where he'd been snoozing. Sadie was in the kitchen with wet hair and fresh clothing. He hadn't even heard the shower kick on. His eyes were dry and itchy and his mouth was like cotton.

"I didn't mean to wake you," Sadie said.

"No, it's okay. I need to get up anyway. I can make coffee."

"I can do it. If you don't mind me rummaging around your kitchen. I noticed you have top-notch appliances and cookware." She pointed to the pots hanging over the island. He'd cut corners elsewhere in order to have the best of the best when it came to his kitchen.

"No, I don't mind at all." It was kind of nice not having to do it, if he were honest. Cocoa bumped his hand for morning love and he scratched his ears and kissed his furry head then let him out to do his business. He turned to Sadie. "Do you usually make your dough at home or at the food truck?" She'd mentioned needing to make it fresh and he'd meant it when he said he'd give her a hand.

"Typically at home. But since it's nothing but charred remains..." Her lip quivered. Her home was gone and most everything inside was either ruined or damaged.

Her eyes were red and puffy. "How are you, Sadie? Really? Don't give me a pat answer or one word like *fine* or *good* or *hanging in there*."

"*Hanging in there* is three words. You that bad at math?" she teased. More teasing to mask the overwhelming feelings underneath. Couldn't blame her.

"Well, well, on no sleep and before sunrise and Sadie Owens gots jokes." He would let her cope in her own way and not push. If Sadie wanted to talk to him, she would. It might be that she simply didn't want to share those kinds of private feelings—her heartache—with him, who wasn't a stranger but not part of her inner circle like Laurie. While he understood, it needled him a little. He wanted Sadie to feel comfortable enough to share her pain with him.

The real question was why did he want that? Was he in the market for a new friend? Or was it something else? Something he didn't want or have time to ponder.

"Right now, I'm okay. I'm focusing on my customers and I'll deal with the house later. I have a million calls to make but first things first." The coffeepot beeped and she pointed to it. "Coffee and my Bible reading. Then I'll be ready to truly start my day. I feel like I need to be prepared and the only way I know how to do that is to spend time with the Lord first."

Rocco nodded. "My Luna always had her Bible beside her and I remember spending the night with her and she would always say, 'The best time to start the day with the Lord is when He brings up the sun.'"

"Your grandma gives good advice." She poured a cup of coffee and stirred in some milk and sugar.

"I have a screened-in porch and there's lighting out there. If you want to watch the sunrise. It's probably not too cold this early but I have a few quilts out there Luna made."

"That sounds like a dream. I always wanted a screened-in porch or sunroom. Thank you for all this hospitality. It means so much. You're sure you don't mind taking me to my food truck? I have what I need there."

"Happy to. I'm going to take a quick shower. Wakes me up so I can concentrate on reading my own Word."

"I saw a worn leather Bible by your recliner."

"Luna's."

"Did she pass?"

"No. She's still strong as ever and full of herself. But she's no spring chicken either and needed a larger-print Bible to read. She gave me hers. I love the notes and prayers she penciled in the margins. All the wisdom God revealed to her and the way she loved her family. She's amazing."

"I hope Myles says those same things about me when he's an adult."

"I have no doubt he will." He excused himself and after cleaning up and dressing in jeans and a solid black T-shirt, he followed the scent of freshly brewed caffeine calling his name. He poured himself a cup, adding only cream. Sadie sat on the back porch with the lamplight illuminating her blond hair like a glowing halo around her.

But someone wanted her dead. Why?

He carried his cup to his recliner and eased into it. Cocoa climbed into his bed, circling then curling up. He knew the routine. Rocco grabbed the old leather-bound Bible and opened it, picking up where he'd left off. In Second John, but his mind swirled with questions and he cycled them into prayers for wisdom and guidance on the RMK case and this new one.

As he was ending his quiet time, the sound of little feet and claws clicking along hardwood drew his and Cocoa's attention.

Myles entered, his soft brown hair in disarray from sleep. He rubbed his tired eyes, big and brown and sweet. He wore Thomas the Train pajamas and a crease from his pillow ran along his left cheek, which was rosier than his right one. "My mommy here?"

"Yeah, Tiger, she is. But she's reading her Bible right now. You still sleepy?"

He nodded and without asking or without hesitation, he crawled into Rocco's lap and laid his head on his chest. He was still warm from sleep. Dolly sat beside the recliner and Rocco patted her red silky head. "Hey, girl." She probably needed to go out but she sat patiently and Myles was already back asleep.

Rocco nestled him closer and ran his hand through his cap of hair, cut in a little bowl cut that suited him, giving him more of a baby look than that of a big boy. Maybe that was Sadie's goal. To keep him little a bit longer. He heard that often from parents—kids grew up too fast. Memories of snuggling with his own father surfaced and the ache in his chest for him flooded in with the past. He missed the old man. As a child, Rocco had seen Dad as big and strong, and he'd never once thought his father would ever die. He was a force to be reckoned with.

But his heart had given out anyway.

It had been unexpected, shocking, and rocked the community as well as their family. He'd lost his grandfather only a few years earlier. Now, only the matriarchs remained. Rocco was truly the head of his family now. The only son. He had three sisters but none of them lived in Wyoming anymore. Jobs and husbands had taken them to Chicago, Memphis and Scottsdale.

When winter hit, he always took a trip to Arizona. Even Memphis and Chicago winters had nothing on a Wyoming winter. He shivered at the thought and listened to Myles's rhythmic breathing. Sweat curled the boy's bangs and the hair around his temples. He squirmed and whimpered.

Dolly sniffed and rose, putting her front legs on Rocco and licking Myles's head, then pawing Rocco.

"What is it, girl?"

Dolly raced through the living room and to the kitchen table where a Thomas the Train backpack hung. Dolly worked the backpack from the chair and pawed inside, retrieving a little white machine.

A glucose monitor.

She raced it to the screened-in porch door and barked.

Sadie jumped up and rushed inside, taking the monitor from the dog and snatching the bag. "Good girl. Good girl." She scooped her son up and brought him to the couch. "Hey, bud, your blood sugar is low. Yeah, you're sweating. Poor baby. Let's get you fixed up." She opened up a container of cake icing and a plastic spoon. "Here, baby."

Myles took the spoon and ate the chocolate frosting.

"Good?"

"I like frosting."

"Not every little boy can have this for breakfast."

She monitored his sugar levels with the machine and in a few moments the sweating stopped and Myles seemed more alert.

"I didn't realize what was happening. I thought he was simply exhausted. I feel bad."

"Don't. It's hard to tell at times, which is why I have Dolly. I don't always know either. But he'll be fine. He takes regular insulin and I keep sugary treats in the backpack and orange juice on hand."

"I don't have OJ but I'll pick some up today."

"You don't have to do that. Frosting works."

"I like chocolate," Myles said.

"Me too, Tiger. But I'll have juice here for you." He tossed a don't-argue face to Sadie and she simply nodded her thanks. Whatever Myles needed, he would have. End of story.

She kissed his sweaty head and Dolly licked his foot. "How does she know when his sugar drops?"

"She can smell it through his sweat. She's trained to know the smell of his sweat—and the chemicals in it—when his blood sugar is fine and when it's low. She alerts by licking him and then getting me the monitor. Dolly is very protective of him."

"That's amazing. Dogs are truly gifted."

She grinned, nodding her chin toward Cocoa. "Like he can detect accelerant."

"Exactly. Saving lives in different ways but heroes none the less."

"I couldn't agree more." Sadie monitored Myles and when he evened out she left for the bathroom to clean up. Myles quietly played with his green and blue train, using Dolly as railroad tracks. Cocoa watched with interest but kept his distance so as to not become part of the railroad system himself. Rocco rubbed his head and laughed.

When Myles perked up and rushed off to explore the house with Dolly, Sadie returned with a sober expression. "Do you think I'm safe?"

Rocco didn't want to terrify her but she deserved his honest answer.

"I think it'll be best to tread with caution, Sadie. This guy wants you dead. He's proven he's not going to back down." But neither was Rocco.

# FOUR

Sadie hadn't been able to free herself from Rocco's ominous answer earlier this morning. After dressing Myles, she re-packed his bag and they dropped him off at Laurie's house. This morning he wasn't as clingy and was excited to be with his sitter, especially since Laurie had promised to buy him a new train. The kid would do somersaults for another train. It was the way to his little heart.

Then Rocco drove her to her house for the food truck, which she'd parked on the street and had been safe from the fire. She thanked God for that saving grace. As they pulled down the street, the smell of smoke lingered in the air and seeped into the car from the vents.

They took the curve and her home came into view. Charred, ashy remains. A burnt shell left testifying to what had once been. Tears surfaced and she didn't bother to hide them. This was total devastation. Utter loss. The truth was she had what was most important to her. Her son. And Dolly. Their lives. Stuff was simply that—stuff. But it didn't erase the deep pit in her chest. Someone had maliciously robbed her of tangible mementos and the evidence of happy times. He'd stolen her home—a place of security and safety.

Rocco clasped her hand in his. "I'm so sorry, Sadie. I

wish there was more I could do. Wish I'd driven by earlier and caught him before he lit it up."

"This isn't your fault. You saved us. Saved Myles and Dolly. I can never repay you for that." She clambered out of the car and stood staring at the heap. From last night's report, the place was no longer structurally sound, but if they were careful she could go through it to see if anything was salvageable. "I had a fire safe in my bedroom with birth certificates, other important papers. My mother's wedding ring and some old photos. Things like that. I'd like to find it." She at least had those few things left.

"How about you let me do it. I can call out the fire chief or the lieutenant—"

"Brody James?" Brody had been a good friend in high school.

"Yeah. I didn't realize you knew him."

"Oh, yeah. We go way back. He warned me about Aaron. Another time I didn't listen. Aaron cheated on me twice that I know about." She sighed and walked around the side of the house where she'd tried to break into Myles's window. Chill bumps broke out along her skin. Without Rocco this would have been a whole different story.

"I guess we should get going. Are you sure you don't mind looking for my fire safe?" she asked.

"Of course not. But you're already behind on morning prep. Let's knead and bake some dough, huh?"

"Yeah. I have to deal with the insurance company today too. They're supposed to send out an investigator. As if I'd hit myself and leave my child in a fire. Or pay someone to knock me out. But I know they're doing their jobs. Still, it's an annoyance and inconvenience."

"I hear ya. The police report will go a long way."

That meant a lot. She needed the insurance money. Rocco

followed her as she circled the house, pausing as she looked at the swing set. Two swings, a baby swing, one slide and a small fort. "My dad built that for Myles. I'm glad it didn't burn. I'd like to take it wherever I go but it's probably going to be an apartment. I don't know that I can afford to have the house torn down and rebuild. The amount of work involved gives me hives."

"My dad built me a tree house. I practically lived in that thing. Try to take it day by day, Sadie. I know that sounds insensitive but everything you have to do is overwhelming. You know how you eat an elephant?"

"You don't. It's probably illegal anyway."

Rocco chuckled. "One bite at a time, Sassy Pants."

She loved messing with him. He could take it. Not everyone could. "So the bite we take is knead the dough."

"Exactly." He slung an arm over her shoulder in a united-front gesture. He didn't mean anything romantic by it, but she couldn't help enjoy the warmth and the sense of security in his arms.

As they approached her pink food truck Rocco snorted. "Did your dad paint it pink for you?"

"Yes. Pink is my most favorite color. Except neon pink. I don't care much for that. Blush. Rose gold. Baby pink. I'm all about it. I just knew I was having a girl and made lists of everything pink and then I had Myles and I can't imagine having a girl. I know these days pink and blue shouldn't matter. But Myles legit loves blue. Thomas the Train is blue. So…"

She froze as she saw it.

"What's…" Rocco's gaze landed on her front passenger tire. Flat as a pancake. "Is that a…" He knelt to inspect. "Bullet hole," he said.

A crack of gunfire erupted as a bullet slammed right into the middle of the *a* in the Sadie's Subs sign. Sadie squealed as

Rocco tackled her to the ground and Cocoa crouched next to them. Another shot fired and this time it hit the ground two feet beside them, bits of grass and soil spraying into the air.

"Run!" Rocco hauled her up and bolted behind a large tree, Cocoa following. "We make for the back of the house and through the woods again."

"I'm getting kind of tired of to 'grandmother's house we go,' Officer."

"I tend to agree but it's the way with the most cover. Let's go."

Without waiting for a reply, he dragged her across the side yard toward the back of the house. Another bullet slammed into the swing set. Sadie ducked and slipped into the woods with Rocco and Cocoa.

"How did he know we were here?" Sadie asked. Had they been followed? Had the killer kept vigil over Rocco's house and then trailed them here? If so, it meant he knew that Myles was at Laurie's house. He could get to her baby at any time. Her pulse spiked and she squeezed her eyes shut as they butted up next to a cottonwood tree.

"He probably knows your routine. That's why he flattened the tire first. He knew you were coming for your food truck. You had to pause to see the tire and that gave him a good shot but he's not a great one. He's using whatever means he can to…"

Rocco hesitated.

"To finish the job. That's what you were going to say, wasn't it?"

"I was." He winced. "Sorry."

She wasn't. She didn't want to be lied to or have anything sugarcoated, if for no other reason than her son's life was in jeopardy and she needed all the facts to make informed decisions.

"Do you think he's gone?" she asked.

"Let's wait a beat. That many shots, someone will hear it and it's in the city limits, which makes it illegal. The police station is only two miles away." Rocco called in backup. "We'll wait until Detective Watershed arrives and patrol units. Then we'll be safe to leave the woods."

Again.

Sadie called Laurie and told her to keep her doors locked and not to take Myles out today. Laurie didn't seem too frightened but she was putting on a brave front because one of them had to and right now it was not Sadie.

Once the cavalry arrived, they gave their statements to Detective Watershed.

"How'd you get on the scene so fast?" Rocco asked as Watershed pocketed his notebook.

"I was out. Like to get cake doughnuts while they're fresh from Round n' Go. I never know if the name is for the round doughnuts or how I'm going to end up if I keep eating them." He winked at Sadie and she snickered. Watershed was far from round. More like ripped and granite.

"Oh. Now *I* want doughnuts," Rocco said but he seemed distracted.

"You're free to go now. Holler if you need anything."

Rocco guided Sadie to his truck. "I'll get that tire fixed. In the meantime, what do you want to do about dough for lunch and supper? You want to call it a day?"

"I wish I could." Sadie's head pounded and she wasn't in to serving crowds. What she really wanted to do was high-tail it out of town until this guy was caught. But she had nowhere to go and not a lot of money to stay gone longer than a weekend at a cheap hotel. "I need to work. Not only to keep busy but to keep food on my table and bills paid."

"I understand. We can take the ingredients back to my

place and make the dough there, then pick up the food truck on the way back to Main Street. I know a guy who owes me a favor. Have a new tire on it in no time. And don't worry about the cost. He owes me." Rocco ran his hand through his thick dark hair and looked at the truck. "You got a spare or should I have him tow it?"

"I have a spare."

"I'll put that on and then drive it over to Tony's. I can't believe I'm going to drive a pink truck. I mean, I'm secure in my masculinity but it's pretty girlie. Even for me." He chuckled, and she caught his teasing. He didn't actually mind at all. But Rocco liked to give her a hard time. As her dad would call it, pickin' and flirtin', but she was certain it stopped at picking.

"I appreciate that. I feel like I should do something. I'm freeloading at your place and now you're taking care of my truck and helping me prep for business. Can I at least make you supper tonight?" She grinned. "No meatball subs. I make a mean cheese-stuffed, bacon-wrapped chicken breast with asparagus and a baked potato."

"You had me at cheese-stuffed." Rocco went to work putting on the spare then she drove his truck, following him to Tony's two streets behind Main Street. He promised to have it done before lunch time. Once they loaded his truck with the ingredients from Sadie's Subs, they headed back to Rocco's house.

Sadie only hoped the rest of the day would be uneventful, but with a killer bent on snuffing out her life, she wasn't counting on it.

A couple of hours later, Rocco parked and walked into the Elk Valley PD for a brief meeting with some of his MCK-9 task force members.

"What are you doing here on a Saturday?" Jamie asked.

"Task force meeting. Any updates on the fires?" he asked.

"No, man. I wish there were. All we have is what we had before. I'm looking into the coach's history. He did like to gamble. Maybe he got in too deep and we can connect his gambling to the feedstore owner. Maybe he had a penchant for ponies and horses too," Jamie said as Ben Armstrong approached.

Ben had been in the Young Rancher's Club and been interviewed by Rocco's father as well as Rocco since the recent murders but he didn't have much information. He now worked cattle with his family and volunteered at the Elk Valley Fire Department. "Ben, what are you doing here? I thought we had nothing new," Rocco asked.

Ben shook his head, his gray eyes steely and his jaw set. Ben didn't hit the gym but he was fit from cattle ranching. He'd helped Rocco a time or two on his own fences that had needed mending. Seemed he was a fan of volunteering. Rocco barely had time to do his one job. But he'd earlier helped Sadie knead dough for sandwich bread and prep the sauces. He might have added a few of his own spices into the meatball marinara. He couldn't help himself.

As promised her food truck was delivered to Main Street and the lunch crowd would be starting soon.

"I was just conferring with Jamie. Had some free time."

How? How did he have free time?

"How's Sadie?" Ben asked. "Jamie said this guy's coming after her hard." A divot formed in his brow and his blond eyebrows scrunched together. "Why would anyone want to harm her and the boy?"

"That's what we're trying to figure out." Rocco checked his watch. "Dude, I got a meeting. Let's catch up later. Yeah?"

"Sure. Don't worry, Rocco. We'll find this guy and keep

Sadie safe—and her kid." Ben saluted and Rocco hurried into the conference room with Cocoa. All the K-9 partners were obediently at their handlers' feet.

Chase Rawlston, leader of the MCK-9 task force, sat at the head of the table with file folders in front of him. Next to him sat their tech analyst Isla Jimenez, who lived here in Elk Valley and was also helping him and Detective Watershed hunt down their fire starter.

Ashley Hanson, the rookie on the task force, glanced up and waved. Probably didn't take her long to hop over since her condo was nearby. Her wave caught his good friend Meadow Ames's attention and she grinned. "Well, it's about time, slacker. I had to drive from Glacierville."

"Ha ha." Rocco grinned at her snark.

Officer Hannah Scott laughed, always finding his and Meadow's banter entertaining. "How you been, Rocco?" she asked, her fiery red hair reminding him of the flames that licked away Sadie's home.

"Not too bad. Staying busy."

"You smell like garlic." Meadow raised an eyebrow. "Would that be because you've been with the pretty lady you're protecting?"

His neck flushed hot and he ignored her but the snickers from the other women forced him to respond. "I cook too, but…yeah. I helped her prep for the day. What was I supposed to do?"

Meadow shrugged and Isla winked at him. Rocco was happy to see Isla smile since she'd been having a rough go with attempting to follow her dream to be a foster mom. But someone was out to sabotage her. They just didn't know who yet.

Liana Lightfoot, their head dog trainer, was the only one who didn't laugh but instead focused on scratching Cocoa's ears. The Lab loved her thanks to the dog cookies she always carried. "Chase is going to video-call the rest of the team who are too far or unable to travel today."

They were too scattered along the Rocky Mountain Region to be here in person. Rocco took a seat next to Meadow. Meadow had huge round eyes and a thick fringe of bangs. She looked more schoolteacher than a tough US marshal.

"Rocco, how's the investigation coming with the arsons?" Chase asked and moved his files to the side, his dark eyes lasered in on Rocco. His slightly wavy brown hair was more disheveled than usual.

"We have nothing new to go on right now. We have confirmed he's probably a white male midtwenties to late thirties, using fire as a method of weapon but he's flexible. He's shot at us multiple times and he's not a great shot, which I'm thankful for. We have no idea why he's targeting Sadie Owens and her son, Myles. We have no connections between our first victims, to each other or to Sadie."

"Have you run a search with that MO through ViCAP?" Isla asked.

He glanced at Chase. "No." They hadn't run the methods of operation through the FBI Violent Crimes Apprehension Program.

Chase nodded to Isla. "Do that now. Something might pop that will give you insight into what's going on. If you need anything else from any of us at the Bureau or among the task force, you got it."

"Thanks."

"Turpentine is the fuel source?" Isla asked, her soft brown eyes resting on him as she entered information into the ViCAP.

"Yes."

"Could be quick, could be days. You know how it is."

Did he ever? No one solved a case in a forty-five-minute window but on TV.

"Let's move on to the Rocky Mountain Killer. Everybody on video?" Chased asked and a round of yeses ensued. "One of our suspects, Evan Carr, Naomi's brother, has been unavailable for another interview."

"That's suspicious," Rocco said.

"My sentiments as well. But according to his employees, he hasn't been into the office for a few days. Supposedly out of town on business." Evan owned a successful recruiting company with offices across the Rocky Mountain Region. He'd had a solid alibi ten years ago and had been helpful. He hadn't been on the PD's radar back then other than being the brother of the young woman at the center of the cruel prank at the YRC dance. The fact he was a tall blond who traveled in the region of their victims was a pretty flimsy reason to suspect him. But despite the Carr siblings not being close, Evan *did* have a motive. They needed that interview.

"Hannah and I reinterviewed Paulina Potter, Evan Carr's girlfriend from ten years ago," Chase said.

"She still standing by her and Evan's claim that they were together during the time frame the three victims were shot?" Rocco asked.

"Actually," Hannah said, "she's become a Christian and has felt guilty about her statement back then." Ah, sweet conviction. "She says there was about an hour that she wasn't with Evan. He disappeared—her words, not mine. She doesn't know where he was."

"What about a gun?" Rocco asked. "Was he in possession of one that could shoot 9mm bullets?"

Hannah responded, "No. Paulina still claims she never saw him with one."

But they did know that Ryan York owned a Glock 17,

which might match the slugs found near all the victims. Dude moved out of state not long after the first round of murders and so far, they hadn't been able to pin him down for an interview either. Again, suspicious.

York hadn't been on his dad's radar during the initial murders since he wasn't in the YRC. But recently, the task force had made the connection between his description, which fit their suspect's, his sister's suicide being a possible motive, and the gun registered to him, which could be the murder weapon they'd never found. "Does he have a tattoo like the witness said—the one who spotted the blond man with Cowgirl?" Rocco asked. They'd discovered their suspect had a tattoo of a knife on his forearm.

"He didn't have a tattoo, but we haven't seen York or Carr in a while. Either may have had it inked recently," Chase said. "We talked with Ryan's ex—" Chase flipped through his notes. "A florist. Brooke. She said Ryan could easily become agitated and was prone to erratic behavior, especially after Shelly's death."

Meadow nodded. "And that anger could be toward Seth Jenkins—who dumped Shelly a month before she swallowed a handful of sleeping pills—and his buddies."

"Brooke said that Ryan heard that some of Seth's friends had swayed him to get him to dump Shelly. She said he hated the way Seth and the gang treated the local girls. Love them and leave them. End of story. Real jerks," Hannah added. "Guys. Ugh."

"Right?" Meadow said.

"Hey, now. Don't be lumping every guy into the crummy category. You know the whole 'a few bad apples spoil the bunch' saying," Rocco said and grinned at their jesting. But he sobered remembering that the semiformal had happened just four months after Shelly York died. It could've set Ryan off—perhaps his sister would've attended had she not sadly taken her life.

Hannah bit into an apple she'd been holding. "Well, we know that when Ryan found out about Trevor's prank on Naomi and how the group joined in to humiliate her, Ryan was livid. Like super livid."

"But he was never one to like dogs," Rocco said. He thought of how well-cared-for their stolen labradoodle, Cowgirl, had appeared in the photo the killer had sent. A plush dog bed, a pink collar with her unfortunate new name. "I remember Shelly being upset in class one day because she'd asked for a dog for Christmas and knew she wouldn't get one because Ryan wasn't a fan. But things change. He could have Cowgirl as some kind of twisted memorial to his sister. Who knows?"

"Anything is possible," Chase said.

"I'm on it even now," Isla said. "Still trying to find out where that pink collar with the name KILLER in rhinestones was purchased, but tracking about fifty shops that sell it across the Rocky Mountains and at least twenty shops in a tourist-ski town as large as Sagebrush where she was first spotted with Blond Guy takes a while. I'm working as fast as I can."

"We know you are," Chase said, "and you're doing a great job."

The team all agreed with head nods and words of encouragement.

"Thanks, everyone. It's just Cowgirl's pregnant now, and I worry about her health and whether or not this sicko who's stolen her will care for the puppies properly."

Rocco worried the same thing but so far Cowgirl seemed to have been looked after well. At the very least the killer might take the puppies to a shelter so they could be adopted. Or they'd find her before she gave birth.

They finished up, ran down what they already knew and Chase ended the meeting. It was the thick of the lunch hour. Maybe Sadie could use another pair of hands. He'd enjoyed working with her earlier this morning to prep. The smell of yeast, tomatoes and garlic permeating his kitchen. Might be something he could get used to, in a perfect world. If his attention wasn't focused on the RMK and this new killer in Elk Valley, not to mention Sadie wasn't looking for a relationship either.

He drove straight to the food truck and parked along the curb, hopped out and jogged up to the window. Sadie stood inside but glanced up as he approached. Her typical easy manner was now rigid, wary. He hated that someone had done this to her—forced her to be on guard and afraid.

"I thought you might need some help."

"You gonna bring up meatballs again?"

"Probably. Can I still help?" He grinned and felt a deep pull in his gut. Why did she have to be so pretty and feisty and fun?

"Yeah. You can help. Saturdays are busiest when the farmers market is open. I could use a second pair of hands."

Rocco laughed, tied the apron strings behind his back then washed his hands. He inhaled the scent of sandwiches and caught Cocoa pacing then sitting.

Alerting him.

He'd caught the scent of fire accelerant. Rocco wasn't sure where yet, but Cocoa could smell it from at least a quarter of a mile away. The K-9 stood and paced again, circled and sat.

Definitely catching the scent.

And where there was accelerant—there would soon be fire.

# FIVE

Rocco grabbed Sadie's shoulder. "Stay here."

"What's going on?" she asked, her voice high-pitched.

"Cocoa's alerting. He smells accelerant." Rocco jumped from the back of the food truck to the ground.

Sadie bounded out beside him. "I'm not staying here alone. What if it's some kind of trap to lure you away?"

Rocco didn't think that was the case, but… "Okay, come on." He patted Cocoa's head. "Track." Rocco let the leash out and ran beside his dog as he tracked the accelerant scent. Sadie kept up beside him.

"Wow, he's fast," she said between heavy breaths. "I should take up running again. This is embarrassing."

Rocco grinned but said nothing. His focus was on Cocoa and the threat he was trailing. Cocoa led them across the street into the park they'd been in last night. Kids were everywhere and parents watching them play, people walking their dogs.

"Where's he leading us?" Sadie asked.

"I don't know. But he's never wrong. If he smells accelerant it's because there's flammable liquid to be smelled." Cocoa cut through the park to the south parking lot and paused, sniffed and jetted forward, racing through the rows of cars until he came to a black pickup truck. He circled the vehicle and sat at the truck's tailgate.

"Good boy," Rocco praised and fed him a doggie treat, rewarding him for good work.

"Do you recognize this truck?" Sadie asked as her glance darted around.

"I want to say no but it does seem familiar." It was an older-model Ford. Looked to be a work truck. He'd seen it before. He simply couldn't place where or whom he'd seen driving it. Inside the bed was a silver toolbox, a few gasoline cans and four empty turpentine cans. Could mean something. Could mean nothing. A lot of people used turpentine to strip or thin paint.

Rocco walked around the vehicle and peered through the windows. A pair of black gloves sat on the passenger side and a half bottle of water was in the console, but the interesting fact was the water bottle was likely made of Nalgene, which was a good source to hold chemicals like turpentine and gasoline. But they were popular bottles, so it could be a coincidence.

"Rocco?"

Rocco turned and Ben Armstrong smiled and waved. "You checking out my new old truck? It's a classic. Got it for a dream—sadly due to Herman's passing. His family auctioned off a bunch of his things including this."

That was where he'd seen the truck. It had belonged to Herman Willows, the feedstore owner who'd been burned to death at his home. Herman had loved this old thing and it was worth a lot of money. Guess his family simply wanted to be rid of it.

"Cocoa alerted because you have turpentine—and gasoline—in the bed. And with the fires going on, I wanted to inspect."

Ben tapped the hood. "Yeah, between cutting Mama's grass and mine, it's easier to keep gas cans filled, and now she's got me stripping some old furniture she wants to stain. I think all these projects are her way of keeping me around more often." He grinned. "Well, I should be off. I had to run to the hardware store."

Sadie piped up. "You didn't find what you were looking for?"

Ben's grin fell and he looked at his empty hands. "Oh. Uh, no. I didn't." He shrugged. "Guess I'll be reduced to ordering from the big place that's taken over the world. I try to shop local if I can, though. Well, you two take care. Good job, Cocoa." He patted Cocoa's head and hopped in his truck.

As he pulled away, Rocco sighed. "I thought Cocoa was going to lead us to the killer and we might be able to put these crimes to rest. Should have known it wouldn't be that easy. It rarely ever is."

Sadie kept quiet but nodded. "You know Ben used to run around with my ex, Hunter. Back when they were in junior high and high school. He was always a decent guy. I never understood what he had in common with Hunter. And these days, I wonder what I had in common with my ex as well."

Rocco tucked that information away and they headed back to the food truck where a line was already forming. Maybe one good thing would come from this day—income for Sadie. As he entered the food truck, he felt eyes on them.

But as he scanned the perimeter from the window, no one was there. Just a creepy sensation and a warning in his gut.

"One ham on rye with extra Swiss cheese," Rocco belted out and Sadie went to work. The past two hours had been a rush but she wasn't complaining. Her feet hurt even though her tennis shoes were made for standing long hours.

Seemed like everything hurt today including her brain, which wouldn't stop thinking about Ben Armstrong and the accelerant in his truck that Herman Willows used to drive.

As she'd told Rocco, Ben knew Hunter and had been friends with him. He'd only been a volunteer firefighter for six months. Why did he have accelerant in the park not that far away from Sadie's Subs? These questions rolled around her head while she worked to put together gourmet sandwiches with sides of chips, pickle spears and soft drinks.

She blew off the idea that Ben had anything to do with the fire at her house. After Hunter, she was paranoid about almost every man. Everyone had an underlying motive, a secret agenda. Her ex-husband had cheated on her multiple times in the short time they were together and had tried to convince her she was paranoid. Imagining things. He had a smooth explanation for lipstick on his collar and perfume on his shirt or being out late. When she'd called to check and see if he was at the bowling alley with the guys, he wasn't. But his story had been they decided to sit around a fire instead, drink a few beers. No one else's woman was calling to check up. She should trust him.

Against her better judgment, her father's warnings and her gut, she had. He'd made her look like a fool. No, she had made herself look that way by believing his sorry self. She'd thought a baby might make things better, bring him home more at night and repair their strained relationship, but it hadn't.

He'd never seemed thrilled about a baby, and then, when Myles had been diagnosed, he'd taken a job driving cattle, which put him gone for six months. She'd received the divorce papers through a courier. No point fighting for a marriage that he didn't want. She didn't contest it.

"You get that, Say?" Rocco asked. Only Dad had called

her Say. It did not sound fatherly rolling off Rocco's tongue. It felt…intimate. She wasn't sure how to feel about that in her head. But her heart made its voice clear in the uptick of her pulse and the way her stomach did a corkscrew.

"I didn't. Sorry. My mind is wandering."

"You okay?"

"Yeah. Just…all over the place. Sorry."

"Two Ruebens and a club."

"Got it."

As the lunch crowd cleared, Sadie heard Rocco say, "Well, look who's here! Hey, Tiger."

"Officer Rocco!" Myles shouted. "Me and Dolly came to eat lunch and see Mommy."

"And me too?" he asked.

"And you too," her little man replied. Sadie popped her head through the open window and grinned. "Grilled cheese and cheese curls?"

"Yes!" he said and ran around the truck. Sadie opened the door and scooped him up, hugging him tight. He was the best thing in her life and she couldn't imagine losing him.

"Have you been good for Miss Laurie?"

"I have. But Dolly ate her Pop Tart."

Sadie chuckled. "Dolly does have a sweet tooth, doesn't she?" She kissed his brow and eyed the red Irish setter. "Girl, you know better."

Dolly's ears flipped back and she shot her the side-eye. "Yeah, you know you're wrong." Sadie patted her head and thanked Laurie for bringing Myles by. Some days were long, like Saturdays. "You want a BLT with extra mayo?"

"Do sharks bite?" Laurie asked rhetorically.

Sadie laughed and went to work but Rocco stopped her. "Hey, take a break. I'll make these. You guys go have a seat on that picnic table and I'll bring you lunch. You haven't eaten either. What do you want?"

"You don't have to do this." But she really wanted to spend time with Myles.

"I'm doing it." A little bit of Italian accent popped through. A gift from having grandparents and parents who had been in Italy at one time.

She nodded. "Then thank you. I'll take the meatball sub, and I'll know if you doctor it."

His mischievous grin revealed he'd been thinking of doing that already. She'd never admit it aloud but Rocco was a sensational chef. His chopping skills alone were remarkable. "Why did you go into law enforcement over culinary arts?" she asked without thinking.

He paused, clearly surprised at her random question.

"Sometimes I'm all stream of consciousness. You have to keep up."

His grin set another spray of flutters into her belly.

"Cooking is therapy but helping gain justice and bringing law and order felt like an honorable calling. To follow my dad's footsteps meant everything to me. And after Seth, Aaron and Brad's murders...when I saw how it broke our community, I wanted to be a part of repairing the cracks. But I did think about it. I thought about owning my own Italian bistro right here in little Elk Valley and maybe expanding. I tell myself when I retire from the force, I might just do it. You want some competition?" he teased.

She laughed. "I'm an Elk Valley staple. Bring it on."

He returned the laugh at her teasing.

"I'm actually trying to launch a catering business," she said. "I have a big wedding to do in the winter for the mayor's daughter and if it goes well, word spreads and it could help me financially."

"I wish you the best. You'll be great at it. I can't imagine you not being successful." He pointed to a bench under a shade tree where Laurie and Myles sat. "Go on. I got this."

She nodded and headed over to the bench, where Myles had laid out a Thomas plastic activity mat and was playing pretend with his trains.

"He seems at home in the truck, cooking," Laurie offered with a twinkle of mischief in her eyes.

"He's a great cook and a pretty great guy but don't tell him I said that." She snickered. Rocco had been a source of comfort and safety for her since the fire, and it reminded her how alone she'd been, doing it all. Being everything. She was the only source of income, which meant she didn't have time to be sick or take a spa day or lollygag. She was the provider, the boo-boo fixer, the problem solver. Cook, cleaner and everything in between. The buck stopped with her for every decision. And she was flat worn out, but God had given her grace each day. Some days she wasn't sure she'd have enough. She was stretched ridiculously thin but somehow she made it through the day even if her head hit the pillow in utter exhaustion.

With all these new fiery trials—literally—she wondered if God had dropped the ball on her. Hadn't her faith been tested enough in the recent years? She could use a reprieve, a season of peace. But no peaceful season had come yet. In fact, it appeared that things had grown worse, and she wondered if she'd messed up or disappointed God somehow. Had she not been faithful enough? Had she not served enough or done enough? Deep down she knew God didn't play tit for tat but it sure felt like that lately.

"You know," Laurie said, "if you're in the market for a good man and I feel like you are—"

"I'm not." Many Elk Valley residents had tried to set her

up with someone they thought was amazing but they hadn't gone through everything Sadie had. She'd been duped by a guy she thought was fantastic. He wasn't. He was the opposite of fantastic. She'd been set up with men who were not at all amazing and she had a hard time trusting. If Myles's own father didn't want him due to his manageable condition then why would a man who didn't share his DNA want to be saddled with medical bills and the responsibility of a small but very active little boy? "And anyway, Rocco has a one-track mind…well two-track. One, his job, especially finding the RMK, and two, his food. Which we do share interests in but that just makes him a friend I have something in common with."

"If you say so. I'm not pushing a man on you. I'm not one of those who think every woman needs a man. I don't. You're strong and independent and can make a life without one, but having a partner to share that life and work as a team with… even I want that, Sadie. You-know-who was a piece of work but not every man is going to be a tragic failure."

"I know." They chatted about other things and Rocco brought them their sandwiches.

"These look amazing," Laurie said. "A man who can cook is a hot commodity. Why are you still single?" she asked.

Sadie's cheeks flushed and she tossed Laurie a glance to warn her to back off. She didn't need a matchmaker.

"Oh, I work a lot for one. And maybe I just haven't met the right lady. Why—you offering?" he teased, and if Sadie were a dog, her hackles would be raised. Was he flirting with her best friend? And should it bother her that much? She'd literally just told Laurie she wasn't interested and had no claim staked.

Laurie laughed at his joke but didn't answer.

"You ladies enjoy. Myles, how's the grilled cheese?"

Myles had already eaten the middle out of his sandwich. "It's good, Officer Rocco."

Rocco rustled his hair. "Awesome. You let me know if you need anything else." He strutted back to the food truck and Sadie and Laurie finished their meal talking about other things that didn't include romance.

Sadie played with Myles and then kissed his cheek. "I'll pick you up after the supper shift, okay?"

"And we'll stay with Officer Rocco again?" His voice held more excitement than Sadie wanted. He'd bonded with the man and she didn't want him to get hurt when things went back to normal. If they went back to normal.

"Yes, just for a few nights and then we'll have to stay somewhere that's just our place."

"But not our house because the fire ate it." His little voice was matter-of-fact but not afraid and she was thankful for that.

"Right. We'll get a new house and new yard and new Thomas sheets. Sound good?"

He nodded and she wiped the shimmer from his grilled cheese off the corner of his mouth. When they left, she sat on the bench for a moment to breathe and to pray. She opened her eyes as a chill swept over her, feeling the awareness of being watched. Main Street was bumping with people and she didn't see anyone openly gawking, but the sensation didn't lift.

She was being watched.

# SIX

Rocco handed Sadie the keys to her food truck after he locked up. She was making him supper tonight, and while it wasn't a date but a thank-you for all he'd done—which he didn't think she needed to do—it felt a little like a date. Truth be told, if he was going to date—and he wasn't—Sadie would be at the top of his list, but a woman like her deserved his undivided attention and he had none to spare with the cases looming over him, consuming nearly every moment. "I need to run to the grocery store and then pick up Myles from Laurie's."

"Would you want to take my vehicle? I can drive the food truck back to my house. Or hitch a ride with Detective Watershed." The Elk Valley PD wasn't but up the street a few blocks. He could use the night air to clear his head anyway. "Plus we need to talk about the case. Really. No trouble."

"You sure?" she asked.

"Positive. Brakes need to be tapped gently or you'll give yourself whiplash."

She grinned. "Noted." She accepted his keys and waved, but he noticed her wariness in the way she scoured the surroundings and her hurried step to his truck.

"Hey, did you get spooked earlier or are you being cautious?" he asked and darted his glance upon the quieter streets. Not much going on after supper on Main Street in Elk Valley. That was small-town life. But they were setting up for a movie in the park night. Once a month until school started they showed family-friendly movies. People brought out blankets and lawn chairs, coolers of drinks and the Parks and Recreation crew popped popcorn for free.

"Both, I guess. I'm just going to the corner market, though. I should be safe."

"Okay, then." He watched her drive away and tried to keep from feeling anxious.

"You working two jobs, now?" Ben Armstrong asked as he approached, carrying one end of a large red cooler. Bobby Linton, another old classmate, carried the other end, a smirk playing on his lips.

"Hey, Ben. Bobby. Yeah, I'm off today, so I thought I'd help her out. Lot going on."

"With the fire taking her house, I can see that," Ben said.

"Any idea who's wreaking havoc across Elk Valley?" Bobby asked and wiped his weathered brow. "Talk is someone wants to burn the whole town to the ground as a protest to not finding the Rocky Mountain Killer. But I don't buy that."

People talked. They had good guesses and ludicrous thoughts about the arsons/murders. "Not a fan of rumors." Rocco nodded at the cooler. "What are you two doing?"

"Drinks for the movie night. Free water and juice boxes for the kids." Ben grinned. "Roped Bobby into helping when he was leaving the hardware store." He pointed to Bobby as if he'd suckered him into doing a good thing for a good cause.

"I don't mind. Not really. The town didn't do cool stuff like this when I was a kid. Or maybe I just didn't know about it. Non-perks of growing up in a boys' home. But Mr.

Landry—the boys' home manager—is making sure they get to come tonight. Get a chance to do real kid stuff."

"That's commendable."

Ben pointed to the food truck. "I saw Sadie drive off in your truck. That going somewhere?" He waggled his eyebrows and Bobby grimaced. Ben at times still acted like a sixteen-year-old teenager with raging hormones instead of his almost thirty-year-old age.

"We're friends and I'm looking out for her. Someone is trying to kill her."

"Her food's not that bad," Ben joked. But neither Rocco nor Bobby found it humorous.

Ben's cheeks reddened. "Sorry. Poor taste. Pardon the pun." He chuckled again. "Sorry again."

"Yeah. You sound real sorry."

"Hey, maybe if something progresses you'll have a date for the reunion," Ben said. "You have until October to win her heart. I hear it's made of stone, though."

"Not cool, Ben. And again, I hate rumors." Rumors caused trouble, sometimes deadly, and he wondered if maybe these recent fires were all ignited over a rumor.

Rocco wasn't sure having the Elk Valley High School multiyear reunion was a great idea but the alumni committee—and Zoe Jenkins, Seth's sister who was leading the charge—thought it would be a positive event in light of the recent murders. Rocco along with some of the other task force members suspected that news of the reunion might have been the trigger that set off the RMK on this new spree of killings.

"I'm not sure I'm attending the multiyear reunion. With or without a plus-one."

Zoe had plastered fliers all over town. Rocco liked Zoe well enough. She also ran a catering company with a focus on dietary needs such as keto, paleo and even diabetic dietary needs. He wondered how she would feel about Sadie starting a catering company.

"We better get these drinks in place," Ben said.

Rocco waved the men on and hopped into Sadie's driver's seat, popped his AirPod in one ear and called Jamie Watershed. He answered on the first ring. "On my way home. Wanted to check in on the arson case."

"I found a connection I'm looking into," Jamie said. "You know Jack Norwood?"

"Yeah. He owns Jack's Bistro and runs two food trucks. He's Sadie's biggest competitor and wants to buy her out."

"She mentioned that. He also tried to buy Herman Willows's property. Prime location to expand his business, but Herman wouldn't sell even though everyone knew he was retiring soon and would have to, but Herman had a beef with Jack. Thought he was a bully and didn't treat people right. Got all this from Herman's daughter who flew in from Orlando to get his things in order. Found a note that said under no circumstances was she to sell to Jack Norwood. Guess who came calling before she had time to even unpack her things?"

"Jack."

"Yup. He's ready to build now and asked if she'd sell."

"What did she say?"

"She said she hadn't had time to grieve and wasn't selling. But it's funny that just a few years ago, Jack's Bistro burned down and they never could determine if it was malicious intent so they paid out."

"And then he purchased two food trucks after he made repairs. Smells fishy."

"Granted the accelerant wasn't turpentine but gasoline. Still, it does indeed stink."

"Can you connect him to the coach?"

"Not as of now, but I know Coach has about ten acres near the foot of the Laramie Mountains. Make a real nice restaurant with a pretty view. I'll see who owns the land now that he's deceased."

Rocco hoped they were a step closer in finding the killer. "I don't know how burning down Sadie's house would benefit him."

"Burning her house down wouldn't. Unless it puts her over the edge financially and he wants her to sell her business to him for a big amount of cash. Or maybe he just wanted her out of the way because she's a competitor. Burning the house is a coward's way out, Rocco. He didn't have to get up close and personal. Hear her scream or beg."

"None of this will gain us a warrant to search his property for turpentine."

"No. But it's a trail to sniff out," Jamie said.

"That it is. I'll talk to Sadie. If anything new pops, let me know."

"Will do."

He ended the call and pulled into his driveway. Sadie hadn't made it home yet. Home. This wasn't her home, but oddly enough, thinking of it that way sent a zing into his chest. A zing he was going to pretend never happened, which meant he didn't need to explore where it had stemmed from.

He went inside, cleaned up and called his mom to check on her and Luna. She said all was well but she'd love to see him. She didn't see him enough. He tried to stop by at least once a week but with the task force and this arson/murder case, he was stretched thin already. But family was everything. He promised to come over in the next day or two.

After he got off the phone, Sadie arrived in his truck. She and Myles bounded out with Dolly and a couple bags of groceries in each of Sadie's arms. Rocco rushed out to aid her. Cocoa raced behind him to Dolly. They'd made friends, and tails wagging, were happy to see one another.

"Officer Rocco, Mommy is cooking us supper. It's going to be yummy too."

"I believe it will," he said as Myles sprinted into the house ahead of him, Sadie calling out for him to stop running through Rocco's house, he was a guest.

"Ah, let him run. He's a boy and boys need to rip and tear."

"They also need to be polite, respectful and mind."

"Fair enough." He placed the groceries on the counter.

Sadie began unpacking the bags as Myles carried his trains to the living room, Dolly and Cocoa following him.

"You sure you want to cook?" he asked. "It's been a tough day."

"I'm used to it, and I never grow tired of cooking."

"All right then. Bring on the chicken. Can I do anything?"

"Nope."

"Also, you're cooking in my kitchen and sleeping in my guest room. You can drop calling me 'Officer.'"

"I could," she said nonchalantly as she washed her hands and looked around his state-of-the-art kitchen. "I need a knife."

"For cooking or you planning to cut my throat?" he teased.

"I am a multitasker. My marinara had sugar in it and extra basil. You did that." She ran her finger across her neck in a slicing motion.

He winced. "Are you mad?"

"No. I expected it." She smirked. "You're so predictable. But my recipes are my recipes. Capisce?"

"Capisce."

He chuckled, loving her sense of humor as he showed her the knife drawer. Sadie went to work slicing then mixing up a cheese mixture with spinach for the chicken breasts. "Who taught you to cook?" he asked, wanting to know more about her. Everything about her, to be honest.

"My dad. My mom wasn't much of a culinary genius and she died before I was in middle school, so all I had was him. My grandmother flew out some and we'd bake cookies."

"The chocolate chunk with pecans you sell at the food truck?"

She grinned and began slicing the chicken breasts open. "You know it."

"Choo choo!" Myles hollered from the living room. "All aboard!" Myles use the dogs as train tracks, gently racing little trains through their fur.

"So I saw a flier today for the multiyear reunion," Sadie said and continued stuffing the spinach and cheese mixture into the center of the chicken breasts. "Do you think it's a good idea?"

"Zoe means well. I'm sure it's sort of a memorial to her brother Seth. I can't imagine what she's gone through."

Sadie nodded. "I heard a rumor—and I know you hate rumors—that Trevor Gage might be the killer's final target since he's the one who invited Naomi Carr-Cavanaugh to the Valentine's Day dance under false pretenses."

The note the killer had left behind mentioned saving the best for last.

Sadie wrapped strips of bacon around the chicken breasts. "Granted, they didn't deserve to be murdered but those guys were ruthless bullies, and they weren't the only ones. Last month, Lee Chambers and Roland Piedmont totally harassed Bobby Linton for looking at Lee's girlfriend while watching the soft ball game."

Rocco frowned. "Lee's always thought women were his property."

"He's a total tool. I felt bad for Bobby and offered him free nachos. Least I could do, you know? And then Lee had the nerve to ask me for free nachos. I was like never gonna happen and told him what I thought of his bratty ways and to grow up."

Rocco grinned. "How did Lee take that?"

"About how you'd expect. Thing is, Bobby actually wasn't looking at Lee's girlfriend—Andrea. I'm not even sure he's still dating her. But anyway, my point is Lee could have easily been a target. On the other hand, Trevor never seemed to be a bad guy in school. I think maybe he did like Naomi and it wasn't a big joke on his part."

Rocco'd wondered the same. "We have task force members in place all over the Rockies. They'll keep an eye on Trevor." And Trevor should watch his back.

Sadie popped the baking dish of stuffed chicken in the oven underneath the roasting asparagus. Then they sat around the kitchen island talking about everything, which came easily. Too easily. And that terrified him.

Sadie hoped Rocco would enjoy supper. She'd certainly enjoyed talking about their childhoods and families and their faith. Conversation wasn't constrained and there had never been a single sliver of uncomfortable silence between them. Banter with Rocco was fun and effortless. She couldn't ever remember a time when discussions were this easy with Hunter or any man she'd dated.

At some point, she'd throw him a bone and call him Rocco instead of officer, but it was simply too fun refusing to do it. She pulled the two sheet pans from the oven and the three baked potatoes wrapped in foil and called Myles, who was explaining the names of all the trains and which ones were grumpy, fun and silly. Rocco was being a trouper, pretending to be fully engaged. The man had a lot on his plate right now.

So did she.

Why couldn't life be like Thomas the Train barreling down tracks without a care in the world? Life was like a track if the track was bumpy and messy. Oftentimes she'd jumped it and gone off the rails. She was especially thankful that God was a merciful conductor.

"Smells awesome," Rocco said, entering the kitchen with Myles on his shoulders.

"Mommy, Officer Rocco is my train. Choo choo! We're heading to the handwashing station! All aboard," he hollered and Rocco sped him around the island twice and then to the sink to wash their hands for supper.

"You been around many littles before?" she asked. He was good with kids.

"I have two nieces and three nephews but I don't see them as often as I'd like. I need to take a vacation and visit. But I like kids. They're honest. I see so much dishonesty in my line of work. It can be souring."

"I imagine so."

As Rocco helped Myles scrub his hands, she found solid white plates in the cupboard and set the table. Then she brought the food to the table and they helped themselves to a delicious supper. Rocco was particular about food, so Sadie wasn't as confident as she'd normally be. He took a bite, closed his eyes and chewed slowly. When he opened them and swallowed, he grinned. "You should be selling this."

Sadie's heart warmed. "You think? I'm making it as a sample of one of three for the mayor's daughter's wedding. I think it makes a pretty dish and we'll do a wild rice instead of a potato to dress it up more."

"It'll be perfect."

That was exactly what she needed to hear. A few words of encouragement breathed hope into her wilted sails. "You know I almost pooh-poohed the idea of going into the catering business since Zoe Jenkins caters. But she does so much specialty food that I thought the two of us could fit into one small town, and I'm willing to travel counties given they pay me. Zoe gave me her blessing and best wishes and asked me to help with the food for the alumni reunion, to which I said yes, so I'll at least be there in a serving capacity. She's really great."

Rocco forked another bite of his chicken and nodded. "I'm glad you're pursuing it. This meal will be a big hit."

"I like chicken nuggets best," Myles added to the conversation but he was scarfing down his chicken, which she'd cut up for him before giving him a plate. Dolly sat hoping for a crumb and Cocoa must have the same idea. He was perched next to Rocco nearly salivating.

"I know you do, bud. Once supper is over, it's bath and bedtime."

"Will you read me a bedtime story?"

"Of course I will and maybe even two or three."

Myles's grin lit her up like a Christmas tree. He was such a special boy. Hunter missed out by choice and her dad was missing out with no choice. Myles deserved a male role model that was stable in his life…but that was the thing. No one was guaranteed tomorrow.

After they finished eating, Rocco wouldn't let Sadie touch a single dish. She cooked and he would clean. He'd mentioned several times how great the meal was and he appreciated her cooking when the day had been so long. It was nice to be appreciated and thought well of. And it gave her time to play boats with Myles while he took a bath.

She dried him off and put him in his Thomas pj's that

Laurie had purchased earlier. Then they trotted with Dolly on their heels to the guest room. Myles had already picked out three Thomas books—no surprise there. She read the first one and by book two his eyes had grown heavy. By the third book, he was sleeping sweetly. She patted Dolly, who lay at the foot of the bed, and slipped out of the room in time to hear Rocco's police radio alert.

"There's a 10-72 at 2569 Main Street…"

Rocco's face blanched and he caught her eye.

"What is it? What's a 10-72?" she whispered.

His expression grew even more dim. "It's a fire and it's at Isla's house."

# SEVEN

Rocco pulled up behind two squad cars and Detective Jamie Watershed's unmarked vehicle, though Isla's house sat directly across from the Elk Valley PD. Two fire trucks were already in position, their powerful hoses gushing water and drenching Isla's small bungalow home.

Where was Isla?

Had she been hurt? Could this arson be connected to the current cases or was the person who was trying to ruin Isla's life responsible? Someone had a grudge against her and was playing dirty. She'd come up with possible suspects but had crossed them all off her list. So who was trying to sabotage her?

She'd been searching for connections on the Fire Man case and running the MO through ViCAP. Could the killer have found out this information? If so, how? Only Jamie Watershed knew this as well as Rocco's task force members.

And anyone that they might have told.

Could this have been a strategic move to keep Isla from investigating? The thought sent his heart lurching. Then he spotted her with a blanket draped over her shoulders. Her brown hair up in a bun and standing with Jamie. Rocco jogged through the crowd of neighbors and the local news vans until he reached them.

Rocco swallowed Isla in a hug and her big doe eyes filled with tears. The poor woman had been through it the past several months. From someone calling in false information that she was unfit to be a foster mother, to her credit cards being canceled. Now this. It was like she was losing everything she ever wanted. How much more could one human being take? "It'll be okay, Isla."

"Will it, Rocco? I'm beginning to wonder."

"Can you tell me what happened?" he asked. Jamie nodded at him and ran off to talk to the fire chief.

"I got home late from the grocery store. Made supper and worked a little, looking to see if anything popped anywhere else on the Fire Man's MO. Nothing yet. I fell asleep on my office futon and woke up, smelling smoke. I climbed out the window and called 911."

"Did you see anyone? Hear anything?"

She shook her head. Unlike Sadie, the killer hadn't attacked her when she'd escaped through the window. The other victims hadn't been physically hurt either—but then they hadn't made it out of the house. Only Sadie and Isla had. One attacked and one not. Why? Could they be dealing with more than one arsonist? He prayed that wasn't the case. But nothing made sense.

"Do you have personal or even business connections with Herman Willows from the feedstore, Coach Ed Towers or Jack Norwood?"

"I've eaten at Jack's restaurants and food trucks. I knew the coach. Everyone knew him in some capacity. I don't have a connection to Herman but I'm familiar with him."

Rocco grimaced. Why couldn't he find a single piece of this puzzle? "Come back and stay at my house."

"I can stay at my grandmother's. But thanks." She frowned. "Aren't Sadie and her son staying with you?"

"Yeah, but I have plenty of room. Not that I'm trying to scare you, but Cocoa will be able to track the scent and I doubt your grandma has a sniffer like a dog."

Isla actually smiled. It was soft and kind. Like her. "You make a good point. Just for tonight, okay?"

He nodded then looked at Cocoa. "We have some work to do now that the fire is out." The damage wasn't nearly as extensive as Sadie's, but Isla wasn't getting back inside tonight. "Track, Cocoa." Cocoa darted into Isla's yard, his nose to the ground as he approached and rounded the back of the house where he circled and sat. Cocoa smelled accelerant.

Jamie approached with Ben. Ben was covered in sweat and soot from putting out the fire. "I think this is the point of origin," Rocco said.

"That's Isla's bedroom," Jamie said.

"The killer knows them personally and has been in their homes, has stalked their patterns and sleep routines or prowled around to find the right bedroom. Maybe all three," Rocco added. "I wonder if the accelerant will be turpentine."

"Should know something tomorrow," the fire chief said as he approached. Brody James was in his midthirties, gruff and a big fan of Sadie's Subs. Rocco had seen him eating a Rueben often. He'd been a baseball boy and taken Coach's death hard. He played on the Elk Valley community softball league and still helped on the family ranch. Like Ben, when did the man find the time? "Miss Jimenez escaped by the skin of her teeth. I'd call it a blessing."

"Isla will stay at my house instead of going to her grandma's. I can keep her safe with Cocoa around. We'll deal with what to do next." Rocco shook Jamie's hand and headed back to Isla. "Hey," he said to her. "Scene is cleared. Point of origin is your bedroom. Good thing you slept in the guest room."

Her lip quivered. "I called Granny Annie. She knows

I'm safe and understands why I'm not coming to her house right now."

"What do we need to collect for you to stay the night?" Rocco asked as he texted Sadie and updated her that Isla was coming to the house.

"Nothing. I keep a go bag in my car because you never know. Are you sure I'm not putting you out?" she asked.

"Not at all."

She grabbed the bag and followed him to his ranch. Sadie opened the door and wrapped Isla in a fierce hug. "I've been worried. Are you hurt? Come in. Come in."

Isla entered his house and set her bag on the floor in the entryway. "I'm okay. Just shaken up."

"I understand. Believe me." Sadie led her to the dining room table as if she were the woman of the home, and Rocco didn't *not* like it. He wasn't sure how to respond. "I put on a pot of hot chocolate. Would you like a cup?"

"Yes, please."

"Officer?" she asked and he caught the twinkle in her eye.

"Yes, Miss Owens. I'd love a cup."

She smirked and filled three mugs with hot chocolate then brought them on a tray to the table. "Myles is asleep. Boy sleeps through anything and I'm glad. All this fire talk is scary." She slid Isla and Rocco their mugs.

"Mmm…this is homemade, not a packet," Isla said. "Nice."

"I'm not a fan of the powdered stuff unless I'm in a pinch," Sadie said.

For a few minutes, they talked about the fire and about the leads being dead.

Isla wrapped her hands around her mug. "I can't stop thinking about the baby girl I missed out on fostering because of the lies someone told about me. Who hates me so

much that they'd do that to me? And set my house on fire."
She shook her head. "I can't even imagine."

"Someone you might have helped put away through your
excellent investigative technical skills?" Sadie asked.

"I don't know. I honestly don't." Isla grabbed her phone
and grinned. "But maybe it's not over yet..." She showed
Rocco and Sadie a few photos of a little boy smiling. "Caring Hearts Christian Foster-Adoption Agency knows I'm
working on restoring my reputation and sent me this picture
of him. His name is Enzo."

He looked about two or three to Rocco.

"He's so sweet," Sadie said. "I hope it works out."

"Me too," Rocco added. Isla deserved to be a mom.

"His parental rights will be terminated soon and he needs
a home. I want to provide him with one but I can't figure
out who's messing with me so I can reclaim my good reputation and foster and adopt. It's my dream, you know? And
now I have to deal with the damages to my house and who
knows how long it will take, even if it wasn't as severe as it
could have been."

"Rest assured, Isla. Everything will work out. We'll keep
praying and trusting God. He's in this even if we can't see
it," Rocco said.

Sadie agreed silently but he didn't see much confidence
in her eyes. Was she losing hope?

Jack Norwood leaned against Sadie's car as she came out
of church with Myles and Dolly beside her. Her stomach
plummeted and then anger spiked. Jack didn't attend First
Community Church, which meant he wasn't here for spiritual growth but business growth and that was low-down and
tacky to boot. "Hi, Jack," she said flatly.

"Sadie, I drove by and saw your car. Thought I'd stop by and see if I can help you."

"My church family is taking care of my needs." They'd gone above and beyond for her. "That makes me all good."

"Hey, little man," he said to Myles, ignoring her dismissal of his help. "How was church?"

"I learned about Jesus."

"That's great. Always good to learn about Jesus." Jack's saccharine smile piggybacked his equally saccharine words. Jack Norwood was the farthest thing from a Jesus-follower.

Sadie opened the back door and Dolly jumped in, followed by Myles clambering into his car seat.

"I wanted to make you an offer you can't refuse," Jack said as she buckled Myles into his seat and laid the picture of Noah's ark he'd colored in the floorboard so Dolly wouldn't crumple it. She'd date it when she got back to Rocco's and then add it… Tears welled in her eyes. She no longer had anything to add it to. All Myles's drawings and special crafts she'd saved were gone. Up in smoke. Buried in ash.

She blinked away tears and held it together for both her son and to avoid Jack seeing her utter vulnerability. She turned. "I assure you I can refuse anything. I'm stubborn."

Jack shot her a flashy grin, his thick dark hair perfectly mussed. No one could say Jack wasn't dynamite in the looks department and improved in his middle age. However, his personality was a firework that bombed and left one disappointed they'd invested in buying it and wishing they'd never anticipated a glorious display.

"I know this about you, Sadie. It's one of the things I find intriguing. You won't sell to me, won't date me… I don't get it."

Of course he didn't. Narcissists never understood rejection. "I guess I haven't heard the message in church yet that you're God's gift. When I do, I'll come beating down your door. Sound like a fair deal?"

"Sounds like sarcasm," he replied without appearing to be offended. Too bad. She was trying pretty hard. "Your situation has changed, Sadie. I'm sorry about the fire and I can't imagine what you're going through but I can help you. If you'd sell me Sadie's Subs and the rights to the recipes, you could come out from under your financial stress and have a fresh start for you and the little guy."

"Myles. His name is Myles." Frustration pricked her heart and her tone came out sharp. But she didn't care. "Now is not the time to discuss business, Jack. It's Sunday and I'm trying to enjoy the day. But the truth is it wouldn't matter what day you approached or stalked me… I'm not selling my father's legacy. It's all I have left of him and I love what I do. So does the community. Why would I want to sell it to you when I can do it myself?"

He cocked his head, his dark eyes sparkling. "I thought you might want more time with your son and I hear you're about to start up catering. That's even more time away but with my payout, you'd be able to start up your business debt-free and have enough to spend more time with Myles and work when you want—catering." He splayed his hands and gave her a number that nearly sent her eyes popping out their sockets. "You do want to spend more time with your son, don't you?"

She didn't answer. He made good points, sadly. She did want more time with Myles. Being a working single mom was tough. Debt and mounting bills even tougher. Should she consider this? What if her catering business didn't take off like she hoped? Then what? Her truck and recipes would be Jack's and she'd be unable to use them ever again. Selling meant no going back to it. She'd been praying about what to do next. She needed direction and wisdom and guidance. Was Jack—even in his arrogance—an answer to her prayers? To her financial freedom? Her emotions had her stirred up so much she couldn't hear clearly. She could turn every scripture into something that worked for or against her decisions.

"I'll… I'll consider it. Don't rush me, Jack."

"I would never."

"Yes, you would."

"Would what?" Rocco asked as he approached dressed in khaki pants and a turquoise golf shirt that popped against his Italian bronzed skin. He'd been on church security today. Sad to think churches needed security measures but the world was uncertain and they couldn't be naive.

Jack extended his hand and Rocco shook it. "Oh, just business talk. How's your investigation going? I hear you're hitting dead ends. That's two for two of your cases, isn't it, Manelli?"

Rocco's jaw tightened but then he smiled. "Some puzzles take more work than others. We'll find who did it. Everyone is on my radar, Norwood. Everyone," he stressed.

Jack's eyebrows rose. "You have a good afternoon." He looked at Sadie. "Let's talk soon. Yes? Maybe over supper?"

"Have a nice Sunday, Jack." Sadie ground her teeth and huffed as he walked to his fancy truck that cost more than she made in a year. "That man is insufferable. He needs a good wallop and Jesus."

Rocco chuckled. "He still wants to buy the food truck?"

"Yes, and the recipes. The truth is his offer is downright tantalizing. But something feels off. Maybe it's the fact my dad gave me that business. I'm trying to figure out if I'm being too emotional. If grief is hindering a great opportunity to start fresh and become debt-free and build a little nest egg. I could use that."

"No peace, no go. Better to wait and do nothing than jump the gun with a yes or a no. God will make it clear like only He can." Rocco opened her driver's-side door. "How about lunch? I'm starving and I know this great place right outside of Elk Valley that gives a spectacular view of the Jelm Mountains. It's just southwest of us. They serve chicken nuggets too. All I'm sayin'."

Myles perked up. "I want chicken nuggets!"

"I guess I can't say no to that," Sadie said as her own stomach rumbled.

"Good. I want to run by the house and let Cocoa out, though. Is that cool?"

"Of course. Should we ask Isla?" She didn't go to their church, but she did attend regularly with her grandmother at her church. "She might want to have some company."

"I'll ask but I imagine she'll be spending time with her grandmother after the scare last night."

She nodded. "I'll follow you back to the house."

After letting Cocoa out, they piled into Rocco's truck, including Cocoa. No point leaving him out when he was a working dog and could go into any place. Isla had declined the lunch offer.

The Big Laramie River rolled between the two mountain views, the tops already snowcapped with hints of a soon-coming winter.

As they rounded a sharp curve, Sadie braced herself and noticed Rocco's expression turn grim and his hands grip the wheel tighter.

"What's wrong?" she whispered and turned up the radio to block out their discussion from Myles's little ears.

"I think we're being followed."

"By who?"

"I don't know. But there's a big black truck that's been on

our behind since we rolled out of town. Or I noticed it then. Might have been on us all along and he's getting closer."

Sadie turned around. Myles played trains in his car seat and the dogs lay back lazily. Sadie's stomach sank. The mountain curves were sharp with nothing but rugged ravines on one side and the river on the other. If they were being tailed, this monster had to know a child was inside. What kind of person would hurt a child? How were they going to keep her boy safe? Keep them all safe?

"It might be nothing," Rocco added but his tone was somber.

"I can't see the driver. The windows are tinted. Black trucks aren't exactly uncommon." Sadie didn't know every vehicle in Elk Valley. "I'm nervous."

"I know." Rocco pressed the gas but he couldn't go too fast around these sharp curves. That was dangerous all in itself. "It'll be okay."

He'd been saying that but so far nothing had been okay. Sadie gripped the door of the truck and prayed it wasn't their killer on their tail and that they wouldn't suffer any more pain. But just as she finished her silent prayer, the front of the truck behind them rammed into the back of Rocco's truck.

Sadie shrieked and Myles called out, "Mommy, what was that?" His little voice was shrill with fear.

"Hang on, Tiger," Rocco said. "Someone bumped us is all." He pressed the gas as they rounded a dangerous curve. Signs to slow warned them to bring the speed down, but Rocco didn't. He increased and made the sharp left, veering out of their lane for a moment. Sadie's heart froze as she gaped. The tires squealed on the sharp turn. She glanced in the passenger side mirror.

The truck was close.

Too close.

Closer than it appeared in the mirror. Even the sticker on the mirror said so. The truck rammed them again, sending Sadie's body lurching forward, her seat belt catching her and slicing into the skin on her neck. She inhaled a sharp breath as Myles cried again. "Mommy, I'm scared."

*Me too, baby. Me too.*

# EIGHT

Rocco prayed with all his might. He not only had Sadie and the dogs but also Myles to protect, and the switchbacks were a death trap without having to floor it and keep from being run off the road into a ravine or the river below. "Everyone, hang tight. It's like Thomas the Train," Rocco said through gritted teeth. "When those mean trains tried to push Thomas off the tracks, he was scared but he was safe in the end, remember?" Thankfully, Rocco had paid attention to the show. "Can you be brave like Thomas, Tiger?"

"I can, Officer Rocco. I can. I'm a train and tiger. I choo-choo and I roar!"

"That's my brave boy," Rocco said.

He jerked the wheel to the right and then to the left, trying to weave and avoid the truck from slamming into his again. In the back seat, Myles choo-chooed and roared repeatedly. Next to him, Sadie bit her lip and white-knuckled the side of the door.

The truck came at him again, and this time he swerved into the left lane, rounding the mountain bend when an oncoming semitruck appeared, honking its loud horn.

*Bawmp. Bawwwwwmp!*

Sadie squealed and Rocco glanced into the rearview. The

truck was moving into his spot to keep him from crossing back into the proper lane.

They could be hit head-on.

No chance of surviving that.

The semitruck pulled his horn and Myles, oblivious, choo-chooed. Rocco had seconds to decide. The black truck with tinted windows was now next to him on the right and the semi was going nuts on his horn and trying to brake in the oncoming lane.

Rocco made a hard right on his wheel, ramming into the Ford. He didn't want to push the guy off the mountain, but scare him into speeding up or slowing down to give Rocco space to return to the right lane.

Twenty feet.

Fifteen.

He rammed the truck again and the truck rammed him back, holding him into the left lane.

"Rocco!" Sadie screeched.

Rocco slowed but the truck did as well. Keeping even with him.

Ten feet.

Eight…

He slammed into the truck again and the driver kicked up gravel as he approached the edge of the mountain with no guardrail.

Four feet.

Two…

Rocco slid into the right lane and gunned it, blowing past the truck and narrowly missing the semi. The driver of the semi pulled his horn and let it blow for what seemed minutes.

Sadie slumped in her seat, her hands shaking and chin quivering. Rocco increased speed and shot a glance into the rearview.

The road behind them was open. No truck, but he ate up

the ground anyway, and when he believed they were finally safe, he laid his hand over Sadie's. "We're okay now."

She released a shaky breath and nodded.

"Did we win, Officer Rocco?" Myles asked.

"Yeah, Tiger. You did great."

"You hear that, Mommy? I did great! I'm grrreeeat!" he mimicked Tony the Tiger from the cereal commercial, a still timeless slogan.

They wound up the mountain and reached their destination. A midsized resort lodge with several little cabins nestled into Jelm Mountain. The views were breathtaking and it almost felt like they hadn't been nearly killed.

But they had.

He found a spot in the gravel parking lot and turned off the truck.

Neither of them made a move to exit the vehicle. Rocco waited to follow Sadie's lead. If she needed a breather that lasted ten minutes or two hours, he'd give her that. He couldn't deny he was shaken up too. He'd been responsible for their well-being.

"Are we here? I'm hungry, Mommy."

"Yes. Yes, we're here and you need to eat. Keep your levels strong." Sadie mechanically picked up her purse and went on autopilot. Her eyes vacant. She opened Myles's door and removed him from his car seat then grabbed his backpack and ordered Dolly out of the car. Cocoa trailed behind Rocco.

Before they stepped away from the car he came around and gripped her shoulders and she fell into his chest, her arms wrapping around his waist. He hesitated from the shock. Not the shock of her hugging him, though it was unexpected, but the shock of how it felt having her in his arms, relying on him for comfort and support. For strength and safety. His arms circled her, drawing her tighter to him as a strangled sob escaped her lips.

"We could have died. Myles could have..." She buried her head further into him as if trying to burrow through to the other side, and he held her a few moments.

"I know. We're going to find this guy, Sadie. I'm not going to stop. I'll work day and night for the rest of my life if that's what it takes, but I will find him. I'll make sure you and Myles are safe no matter the cost. You have my word. My promise."

She nodded against his chest.

"Mommy, are you sad?" Myles asked.

Sadie pulled away then, and the vacant space, the coldness of her distance was unsettling. He fought the impulse to pull her back to him.

"No, baby. Let's go inside and order you some chicken nuggets."

Rocco scooped up Myles and they entered the dimly lit establishment, the dogs trailing along beside them. Smells of a charcoal grill, sizzling beef, onions and garlic wafted through the atmosphere, rumbling his empty stomach and promising that for the next hour or so, they'd be happy and protected and could enjoy a meal together. But deep inside, Rocco had a million questions.

Who would have followed them? Why Sadie? Why come after her this hard?

Then he thought of Jack Norwood. He'd been at the church. Said he'd seen Sadie's car while passing by. A more plausible story would be he was following her. And he'd followed them here. She'd all but turned him down in the church parking lot.

Jack wanted things his way and when they didn't go his way...

Rocco followed the hostess, who led them to a nice big

booth in the corner. Both the dogs lay under the table, behaving as they'd been trained. She brought Myles a booster seat to raise him up and he and Sadie sat across from him. He was careful not to bring up the near fatal incident. Little ears listening and all, and quite frankly, for a short time, they needed normalcy. Burgers and fries and ice cream sundaes and small talk, nothing heavy or somber. Anything besides fires and murders.

But at some point they'd leave and march back to reality. And the reality was someone wanted Sadie Owens wiped off the face of the earth. If fire and bullets and car accidents didn't work, Rocco had to anticipate a new line of attack so he could plan a new line of defense while working toward an offensive play.

After perusing the menus, they ordered. Nuggets and fries for Myles and bison burgers with Swiss cheese and mushrooms for him and a bacon bison burger for Sadie. His phone rang.

Jamie Watershed.

He answered. "Hey, Jamie. What do you have for me?"

"Sorry to call on a Sunday. I know it's the Lord's day for you. But we got the report back from Isla's house fire. Accelerant was gasoline not turpentine. Unless he ran out and was in a pinch, which I don't believe, he's probably not the same guy."

"Copycat?" Why? Someone taking advantage of the fires and trying to take out Isla and pin it on the real arsonist/murderer? She'd already had someone gunning for her. Could this be their work as well? Or could it be more sinister? An arctic pit formed in his gut.

"Could be."

Rocco briefed the detective on their close call then they disconnected. Rocco needed to talk to Chase ASAP.

If the fire was a copycatter and it was as nefarious as Rocco imagined, that meant the Rocky Mountain Killer might be in town and targeting Isla because she was coming close to finding him.

Too close.

Sadie had spent most of the morning at the community center preparing the three sample menus she'd offered to the mayor's daughter. Her friend Abby had opened the kitchen to her for free and it meant the world. All Abby had asked for was the leftovers. Sadie had laughed and called it a deal.

Twila Monroe would be here in half an hour. Sadie had made the three meals on a small scale for her and her mother to sample and choose from.

Stuffed chicken breasts with the asparagus and wild rice.

Beef medallions with mushrooms and onions in a béarnaise sauce with new red potatoes and steamed green beans. And the third choice was seared salmon with caper lemon beurre blanc, risotto and market mixed beans.

Sadie thought it was a good assorted choice or she could even do a mash-up if Twila wanted. She'd bend over backwards to be flexible if it meant securing their business, which would then open up opportunity for more catering jobs in the future.

She had the meals in the warming bins waiting until they arrived to plate the food. She was glad for the distraction this morning. Laurie had Myles and her part-time employee, Blanca, was running the food truck until Sadie could arrive.

But in the back of her mind, the arsons and the killer ruled her thoughts.

Rocco was on shift now, but last night he'd helped her set up and prep the food. They'd done it in mostly easy silence. Someone had almost hurt her baby. Since then she'd been working with a continual tremor in her hands, unable to shake the fear. But the thought of Dad made her smile. He would have liked Rocco. Called him full of mettle and grit. Sadie agreed. Not only was he honorable but full of integrity and chivalry. And he was easy on the eyes. Rocco had the body of a twenty-eight-year-old man who worked out hard. And while she shouldn't be concentrating on his physique, she was twenty-six and could admire a set of guns and broad shoulders without the guilt. She simply refused to become emotionally attached, but it wasn't easy separating appreciation from a deep like for the man.

No denying she did deeply like him. It was about impossible not to.

"Hey," his deep voice boomed and she startled. He stood in his Elk Valley PD uniform, Cocoa at his side. His dark scruff gave him an edge, but his dark friendly eyes betrayed that gruffness. "I thought I'd stop by and check on you and wish you the best today. It smells awesome in here."

"Abby called dibs on the leftovers but if you're nice I might consider making you another meal. I owe you."

He shook his head, a lopsided grin forming around the corners of his lips. "You owe me nothing. No keeping score here, but I do have a teensy ulterior motive in coming by." The friendliness was replaced with mischief and his eyes gleamed.

"Oh yeah?"

"Yeah. I didn't think last night was the right time to bring it up—with us almost dying."

Sadie inwardly shuddered. "And what is that?" she asked. "That you now want to bring up?"

"You called me Rocco." His grin spread into a full-blown smile that could solve the world's energy crisis. It definitely powered up her heart.

"I did no such thing."

"Oh, but you did, milady."

She laughed. "Milady? I'll have you know I'm a young, independent woman who is an entrepreneur. No miladies around here." But she loved his sense of humor. "And again, I did not."

He ate up the distance between them and she caught the scent of his soap, with a hint of spice. Looming over her, he held her gaze. "Right when I rammed the truck again, you hollered, 'Rocco!'"

"Well," she said, her throat dry as dust, "that doesn't count. I wasn't thinking."

His eyebrows rose. "You didn't call out 'Officer' but 'Rocco,' which tells me you have to concentrate not to call me my name. I like it. And also, you did say it. Just so you know I know. And now you know I know."

Her eyes were locked on his, completely arrested in his midnight gaze, and her belly was full of delightful flutters. How long had it been since she felt a flutter? She wasn't even sure she had a good comeback, a sassy one-liner. "You don't know anything."

His smile said otherwise. Was her attraction noticeable? Why did he have to be so appealing on every level? Unfair. "I know *that*."

Her insides were shifting and her nerves hummed. Never good. She changed the subject. "Well, since you know so much, what do you know as of today about the arson at Isla's? Was it a copycat? And have you looked into the truck—the make and model—that tried to run us into a ravine yesterday?"

Rocco's smile faded and he pulled back. "We targeted black Fords in the county and it's a lot. We narrowed the make and model to the years between 2010 and 2021. Isla is working on it."

"And Isla?" she asked.

"As far as her case goes, I talked with Chase and Isla this morning and we think it is a copycat. We haven't made the accelerant public."

"Do you think it's the RMK? Here in Elk Valley trying to kill Isla for helping with the case? If that's true, then will you or Chase be next? You both live in Elk Valley."

Rocco frowned. "Chase and I discussed this. We don't think it's the Rocky Mountain Killer. He's been spotted in Sagebrush, Idaho, and his main targets aren't on the task force. Plus, his MO includes announcing that it's him with the notes he stabs into the victims he shoots to death. But someone has it out for Isla, that's obvious, and we think it's that person. It's personal. Whoever it is used the arsons as a way to try and hide, but the accelerant exposed them. But we don't know for sure. It's possible the killer ran out of turpentine—but unlikely. We'll keep looking."

Good. Sadie wanted that guy found. "You might ask around and see if a black Ford had been seen around before the murders of Coach and Herman. If they were being stalked to gather intel on their routines, it could have been in a black Ford with tinted windows. No one would look twice at a truck like that in these parts."

Rocco folded his arms over his chest, his biceps stretching the fabric. "You make a good detective, Owens. I'll ask around. Inconspicuous means out of mind. Someone may have seen it but didn't think it pertinent information. We now know it is."

"That's not detective work, Officer. That's common sense. Anything else I should know before Twila arrives?" She checked her watch. "She's due here in six minutes. I'm nervous now." Her stomach was a ball of raging knots.

"Sadie, you make great food. You're awesome and anyone would be psyched to have you cook for them." He rubbed her shoulders like a coach pepping up a player. "You got this, but more importantly, God's got this. And He's got you."

Didn't really feel like it lately.

"I know." Didn't matter what she felt. Truth was truth. She'd have to walk this one out by faith—unseen. Lean on God's understanding and not her limited knowledge. Because she knew absolutely zipola. "Now, anything else?"

"No, it can wait." His eyes held reservation and concern. He knew something of importance and that was probably his real underlying motive in swinging by.

"If you don't tell me now, I'll worry the whole time wondering. I have a big imagination, Officer, which means I can worry big too."

Rocco expelled a heavy breath. "I did a check on your ex. Hunter's been spotted in town this past week. And he drives a black 2016 Ford. We're still narrowing things, but I wanted to let you know he's here. I have to wonder if he was in town during the July murders. I don't know how he could connect to the other victims but he has a reason for you and Myles to not exist. He might not want to pay child support or he might want sole custody of Myles in order to gain access to any insurance you might have, an inheritance plus property."

Hunter a killer?

If he was desperate for money. His parents had mostly cut him off when he got into so much trouble. Desperate times led to desperate and criminal measures.

# NINE

Sadie finished cleaning up her mess in the community center kitchen and, as promised, delivered on the leftovers for Abby. Twila had gone with all three menu items and a menu card for guests to choose which entrée they desired, and she was paying handsomely for the three choices.

Sadie leaned against the stainless steel kitchen sink with a smile on her lips. In all this upheaval and mess, God had shown her kindness. Every good and perfect gift came from the Father and she was grateful and thankful. This money would be a huge blessing to her and to Myles.

Dozens of decisions needed made. What were they going to do about living arrangements? What would she do about her house? Bulldoze and rebuild—that was super expensive. Sell the property for someone else to bulldoze and build? She hated leaving what was left of her father—the memories in the house. Every now and then she caught his scent of Old Spice. Why did life have to be so hard? Maybe things would look up when the insurance investigator finished his or her findings. She had no idea how long it would take.

She loaded the supplies into her car. Things had run long and it was almost two o' clock. She needed to get to her food truck to take over for the supper shift from Blanca. As she closed the trunk, she had that same eerie suspicion of being watched. She surveyed the area, seeing nothing. A few moms entered the gym for some afternoon exercise. No one lurking creepily, but her gut warned her that she was being spied on.

Who? Why?

"Hey." The voice startled Sadie and she jumped. "Whoa," Lee Chambers said, his beefy hands up in surrender, his blond hair flopping over his sharp blue eyes. He looked more surfer than rancher. "What's got you so freaked out?"

Oh, just a killer trying to take her and Myles out, and the fact it could be her ex-husband now that she knew he was in town and the possible motives Rocco had mentioned. "Just jumpy, I guess. What are you doing here?"

"Swimming laps." He held up his gym bag. "Training for a triathlon in the spring. What are you doing? Aren't you supposed to be manning your food truck?"

Since when did Lee pay attention to her schedule? "I'm catering Twila's wedding reception this winter. She was picking out food choices."

"Nice. Didn't Jack Norwood offer to cater her reception?"

First Sadie heard about it. "I don't know."

"Yeah," he said and nodded. "Talked to him a couple weeks ago. Twila didn't love his menu idea, said his chicken was dry and he had some choice words to say about her. That dude is hilarious."

Yeah, slandering someone took a stroke of comedic genius. Of course, Lee would think it funny. Lee was a notorious jerk and had been since middle school, when he'd realized he was good-looking and agile. Sadie wasn't one to stereotype, but Lee fit the jock bill and took it to new levels.

"Saw your ex by the way."

Sadie's stomach pitched. "You did? When?"

"Yesterday. He was at Moe's."

"Moe Riley?" He was a local mechanic. Owned a garage about three miles from here.

"Yep."

"What time?"

Lee shrugged. "Four or five o' clock. I don't know. Why?"

"No reason." That gave Hunter time to try to kill them and get back to have his truck looked at for repair. Moe often did things off the book. The guy was a little sketchy. "Did Hunter say why he was in town?"

"Clearly the two of you have communication issues." Lee smirked. "All I know is we're gonna hang out one night. Drink a few beers and probably poke at a fire."

Chills scraped her spine. Had Lee used that term absent-mindedly or was he alluding to something more sinister. Was he *poking* at her?

"He's probably going to attend the multiyear reunion in October. I heard from Zoe that you're helping her with the food. I told Hunter he better not eat. Just in case you take the opportunity to poison him." He laughed and when Sadie didn't, he tapped her shoulder lightly. "Sadie, ease up. You take things entirely too seriously and always have." He waved her off before she could respond and strolled across the lot, going inside the community center for his laps.

*Bye, Felicia.* Lee Chambers was a total dillhole.

The sensation of being watched dissipated and she wondered if it was Lee who'd been lurking. Rocco needed this information. In person. She hopped inside her car and drove to Main Street, where a small line awaited a late lunch outside Sadie's Subs. Steady business was always good to see.

Thoughts of business took her mind to Jack Norwood. He'd also given Twila samples and quotes for the food for her wedding. Twila hadn't mentioned it but then why would she? She'd turned him down. That would have irritated Jack.

Twila's wedding was a big deal. She was a big deal, and more importantly, her father—the mayor—was. Losing his business to Sadie wouldn't sit well with Jack. Now Jack wanted to buy her out and had the nerve to show up at her church.

She texted Rocco to swing by after his shift and get a bite to eat. She'd ask him then. Sadie made a quick turkey sandwich then relieved Blanca and went to work on orders until there was a lull. By five, the truck was swarmed but she was prepared and worked nonstop while chatting with customers and serving them, but a sense of foreboding lingered through her veins and those unseen eyes landed squarely on her.

She couldn't flee it.

She itched to run somewhere she couldn't be found, but she had no such place and life had never given her an easy way out.

After plating a meatball sub, she handed it to the customer, took the money and looked up only for her blood to freeze, leaving her lightheaded.

"Lookin' a little scared, Sade." Hunter stood with a crooked grin, his amber eyes piercing hers and his dark hair a little longer than he'd normally worn it. He dressed in faded jeans and a worn gray T-shirt. "Thought I'd grab a bite while in town."

She swallowed hard. "Why are you in town?"

"I grew up here. Have family here. My brother says your house burned down. Drove by. Saw that it had. Myles okay?" he asked as if he actually cared. If he cared about his son he wouldn't have left when things grew tough.

"He's fine. What can I get you? And before you mention it, it's not on the house." Her tone was icy but she didn't care. Hunter was nothing short of a mooch.

He held up a twenty-dollar bill. "I wasn't going to ask. Where you staying since the house burned?"

"What can I get you besides personal information? That's not for sale." She crossed her arms, thankful no one was in line behind him.

"I suppose I deserve the ice queen in you. I'll take a roast beef with extra provolone and an iced tea."

She hurried and fixed his sandwich, tempted to spit in it, but she was a professional. She took his money and handed him the food, tea and a napkin then gave him his change.

"Look, I was wondering if while I'm in town I could see the boy."

"No."

"He's my son."

"You pay me child support? Have you seen him in three and a half years? If either of those answers are yes you can visit him all you'd like while in town. Otherwise, pound sand, Hunter."

His jaw ticked. "I've made some changes in my life, Sade. I know I've made mistakes. Big ones. I'm… I'm considering moving back."

"Good for you. Make sure it's far away from us." Wherever they'd be living. She wasn't sure. Hunter had turned over new leaves several times in their relationship. The resolve never stuck, and now wasn't the time to renew a father-and-son relationship with Myles. It wasn't fair to the kid. Besides, he didn't even know Hunter.

"That's harsh."

"Is it? Walking away because your child is sick is harsh. Not even attempting to help financially is harsh. Not coming to my own father's funeral after all he did for you is harsh. I can keep going. Shall I?" She folded her arms over her chest, which was about to erupt like Vesuvius. Angry lava flowed to the tip of her tongue and everything about turning the other cheek and being kind and any other scripture burned up in its wake.

"No. Look, can we get together tomorrow or the next day. Have a public meal. Talk. Please?"

"What are you driving these days, Hunter?"

His eyes narrowed and he cocked his head. "A black Ford 150. Why?" he asked cautiously.

Sadie's insides turned claustrophobic and she gripped the counter. "I don't see it."

His neck reddened and his nostrils flared. "I had a little fender bender yesterday. Hit some railing. I forgot how sharp the curves can be in Elk Valley."

"Sharp enough to kill someone."

"What does my mode of transportation have to do with us talking?" he asked.

"Because," Rocco suddenly said as he strode up to the food truck, "someone in your make and model tried to run us, with Myles, off the road yesterday afternoon."

"Manelli."

"McLeod."

Hunter glanced from Rocco to Sadie and then repeated the look. "You two together?"

"Would it matter?" Rocco asked. "Where'd you hit that railing?"

Hunter balled a fist. "I didn't run anyone off the road and I would never hurt Sadie or my son." He shot Rocco a scowl. "I'll be back, Sade, when it's more convenient. This is ridiculous. You know me. I've made messes and done some pretty crummy things but I am not a killer. You know this."

Sadie wasn't sure. If Hunter was in debt, and he always was since his parents had cut him off, then anything was possible to not have to pay child support, if he feared her coming for it. But she hadn't. And as Rocco mentioned, he might want to get rid of her in order to secure Myles as a cash cow. But the truth was she didn't have much life insurance and the house wouldn't appraise for high dollars, even if she renovated it. But Hunter didn't know that.

She remained silent and he huffed and stalked across the road toward the park.

"You okay?" Rocco asked.

"Yeah. Just shocked to see him."

"Convenient timing for him to be here, don't you think?"

It was exactly what she thought. If her ex was back, it wasn't for anything good no matter what he claimed.

Hunter McLeod was bad news and always had been.

Rocco had spent the rest of Monday and all day Tuesday tracking down leads to Sadie's case and the previous arsons. He and Detective Watershed also spoke with family members and learned that Jack Norwood had approached Coach Towers wanting to buy some prime property near the foot of the Laramie Mountains, which would make a perfect location for a restaurant, giving that lodge some competition. Jack had offered him more than it was worth but Ed's son, Davis Towers, wasn't interested in selling.

Jack had approached Herman as well as Ed and Sadie about selling. Just this past Sunday he'd tossed out a proposal to buy her food truck and recipes—again. Sadie had turned him down earlier, but with the house fire, his offer was tempting and she'd been considering selling. It would make her financial hardships easier, but she'd lose her father's legacy to her as well as family recipes.

Last night she'd mentioned that everything was up in the air and she feared it wasn't going to land in soft places but come crashing down all around her. He wished he could erase all the bad things that had been transpiring and make sure she had great opportunities for the future. But he'd learned a long time ago that he wasn't God, and jumping in to handle things wasn't always his place. Man, he wanted to, though. He wished he could solve these cases before anyone else got hurt—or died.

Jack Norwood seemed to be the most likely source of the arson, because he had connections and his own restaurant had burned to ash although it hadn't been ruled malicious. Still, that didn't seem like Jack's style. He was sketchy but sketchy was a far cry from a murderer.

He had texted Isla an hour ago while he patrolled his zone, which included Main Street. It was almost lunchtime and he was already heading toward Sadie like muscle memory. These past few days of having her and Myles with him had been pretty epic. He hadn't realized how lonely he'd been in that empty house until it was filled with warmth, humor and a child's laughter. It had felt more like a home than a house.

It was a little past one and the lunch crowd had dwindled which had been his plan. When it came to spending time with Sadie, he didn't want to be rushed. He wanted time. Slow, measured, quality time.

Those feelings scared him a little. He didn't have time to be caught up in a romantic entanglement. And Sadie wouldn't even call him *Rocco*, though he was pretty sure it was more for a joke than for only seeing him as a professional, which was the way it ought to be. Just two professionals helping another out.

That was all it could be. End of story.

He stopped at the window and she reached down and patted Cocoa then looked at him and grinned, sending a wave of whirls through his gut. No. No. No. He did not want this reaction. He had to stay focused on the case. Keep his head and his heart separate. "Hey," he said, keeping it cool like

he wasn't flushed hot inside and his tongue heavy and unsure what to speak.

"Hey. You want that meatball sub with extra marinara,
don't you? Why? Because you love it."

"Only if you use extra fresh basil and switch to Roma tomatoes and add a dash of crushed red pepper and a pinch of
sugar."

"Well, you'll be happy to know I didn't. Don't want to
ruin a good thing."

He raised an eyebrow and she held his gaze. Man, she
was pretty. And sassy. He wasn't sure what he enjoyed more.
Looking at her or hearing her. Maybe hearing her. She was
like a perfect fire-roasted tomato—full of color and flavor
and a kick of spice to life.

"So you want to ruin your sandwich," he said.

"And maybe your day."

He laughed at this. She didn't even crack a smile but the
playfulness in her green eyes was evident. She handed him
a meatball sub in its paper holder, three napkins, an iced tea
and a bag of kettle-cooked chips.

His usual.

She'd had it made and ready.

"How did you know—"

"Because I know things." Her eyebrow arched and he
shook his head and tried to offer her a twenty-dollar bill.

Sadie raised a hand in protest. "Keep it. I'm not paying
you rent. And I've decided you don't really dislike the meal
or you wouldn't order it every time."

He shoved it in the tip jar when she glanced across the
street then he turned to see what had caught her eye. "Maybe
I just like getting under your skin." He glanced across the
street. Lee Chambers was locked into a serious discussion

with Jack Norwood and Ben Armstrong. Jack looked irritated, Lee furious and Ben uncomfortable.

"What do you think is going on over there?" she asked.

"I don't know." Maybe Ben would reveal it later. They were friends. Ben shook Jack's hand and waltzed up the sidewalk while Lee remained, raking a hand through his hair, then Lee finally nodded and stormed away in the opposite direction. He pivoted and made eye contact with Rocco and scowled then kept on walking.

Jack turned and spotted them gawking and hustled across the street. Rocco should cite him for jaywalking. "Well, how's business, Sadie?"

"Fine."

"Given any more thought to my offer?" he asked, his grin whitened by those toothpaste strips and a little too white in Rocco's opinion.

"I'm considering it, Jack. But I need more time. I haven't even heard back from the insurance adjuster. My life is up in the air and I need to think about it for more than three days."

"Fair enough. Can I order a tuna melt?"

"Of course."

"Extra cheese and a pickle?"

"You got it." She went to work and Rocco bit into his sandwich. Needed more basil. He chewed and swallowed then pointed across the street.

"You in the business of ticking off people? Lee looked irritated."

"Lee is always irritated," Jack said and smirked.

He had a valid point.

"He bid on a drywall job at my restaurant. We're expanding. He didn't get it. He was letting me know of my grave mistake."

"And Ben?"

"Ben is mending a fence at my farm. He was at the supply store and asked if he should put his supplies on my account or settle up later."

Jack was being forthcoming with the conversation. A little too forthcoming. Truth be told, nothing they spoke about was Rocco's business. He didn't expect Jack to respond so eagerly and that made him suspicious.

Was Jack lying about the conversation to cover up something else? Or was he telling the truth? His body language didn't indicate lying, but he might simply be that good at deception.

Sadie returned with Jack's order and he handed her a twenty. She made change and he bit into the sandwich. "Good stuff, Sadie. Consider my offer, which includes the recipes for these meals. It's a handsome offer."

"The secret is spitting in the recipe. Enjoy." Sadie returned to the back of the food truck.

Jack eyed the sandwich then tossed it. "Just to be safe," he said and strode down the sidewalk.

Rocco opened the back of the truck and found Sadie sitting on the small bench, her lashes wet with tears.

"Hey, hey," he said gently. He hated seeing women cry, especially Sadie. He sat beside her and put his arm around her shoulders, bringing her closer to him and catching her sweet scent mixed with the spices from cooking. "Don't let Jack Norwood crawl under your skin. You're under his. He tossed the sandwich."

"Like I'd spit in a customer's food. Even a smarmy one." She sighed. "I could use that money he's offering. But at what cost? My dignity? It's like dancing with the enemy and he's stepping all over my toes."

Rocco prayed he'd be able to speak wisdom. He had no clue if she should sell or not. Based on Jack's personality,

Rocco would advise her to tell him to take a hike. But his answer came from emotion not prayer. "I wish I had the answer. I don't. And when I don't know the next step, I stay on the step I'm on until it's clear. I know how hard that is. We want to move, forge ahead and get from point A to B in the quickest pace, but often God makes us wait. Longer than we want or think we need to, but that's one of the ways He builds our faith and our dependency on Him. So my advice is just wait. Don't make any hasty decisions."

"That's good advice."

"That was my Luna's advice when I wanted to plow ahead without any concrete guidance. She's right."

She raised her head and he hadn't realized how close in proximity they were: her nose bumped his and her warm, minty breath swirled around him. Without thinking, he brushed a stray hair stuck to her damp cheek behind her ear.

"She's a smart lady, your Luna," Sadie whispered, holding his gaze and not backing away.

"She is. And so are you." He felt the pull toward her and when his lips brushed against hers he realized it wasn't an invisible tug, but reality. He'd physically moved into her space.

A banging on the side of the truck startled them and Sadie jumped up, her cheeks a deep red. "Sorry," she called and hurried to the window.

What was Rocco thinking? He had no business kissing Sadie Owens. It would be like giving her false hope, and she'd already had enough dreams dashed. He stood and brushed his hands on his thighs. Time to get back to work.

His priority wasn't his heart. It was homicide.

And he had more than one to solve.

# TEN

Sadie watched Myles play with his trains, mimicking the actions on the Thomas show he was watching on Rocco's TV. Earlier today, she'd engaged in a kiss with Rocco. The moment had been intimate and she'd been emotional, but not so much her emotions and brain hadn't been working. He hadn't taken advantage of her in a vulnerable situation.

By calling him Officer she'd hoped to keep some distance between them. That clearly hadn't worked. If a customer hadn't interrupted, she would have allowed the kiss to continue, and if she let herself imagine—which she wouldn't—it would have been an epic kiss.

Now what was she supposed to do? Sadie had too much piled on her plate for love. She'd been burned too many times. She winced at the thought. Last thing Sadie wanted to envision was fire. But it was true. Sadie's judgment in men wasn't always stellar. Aaron Anderson for one and Hunter for two. It was more than that, though.

Did she want to risk someone not being able to handle Myles's medical condition?

What if it became too much for a man to handle? Some days it was too much for her. Dozens of times each day she prayed for God to heal her little boy. He had the power to do it. Why should a sweet little boy suffer? The fact he might always be saddled with this condition seemed unfair and it daily broke her heart.

Yet her little boy was full of joy. He was brave and fearless. He endured injections and doctor visits with grace. And he never failed to remind her that Jesus loved him. The Bible told him so. He wasn't angry and he'd never asked why God hadn't healed him. Never crossed his mind that God might not be good or faithful.

Why didn't Sadie have that unwavering faith—faith of a child?

Easy enough. Life had battered her until her bruised heart stayed black and blue. Her own choices and consequences had thrown her around like a rabid dog with a rag doll in his mouth. Instead of continuing to trust and lean on God, she'd slowly let her faith erode to the point where she questioned and doubted everything.

She wanted that childlike faith back—no spiritual whiplash from doubting then believing fully. She wanted to sing of a "good good Father" in the middle of her own vicious trials. She wanted to be able to say, "I trust Him even if..." and mean it to the marrow of her bones.

"You're in deep thought," Rocco said, leaning on the door from the laundry room to the kitchen where Sadie sat with a cup of chamomile tea, the aroma relaxing her. After she finished the dinner crowd and closed up, she'd picked up Myles and they'd eaten leftovers from the day's cooking. Easy and simple.

After the interrupted kiss, Rocco hadn't said anything about it; his only words were that he'd see her later tonight because he had to work a little longer with Detective Watershed on the arson case. She and Myles had come back here and been puttering around for an hour.

Nerves sent a twisting into her belly. Should they talk

about the kiss? Let it go like it never happened? What if he tried again? Would she have the strength to resist? "Just thinking about things. Faith things. How was the rest of your shift?"

"Uneventful." He undid his police duty belt and gently laid it on the high shelf attached to the small row of cabinets in his laundry room.

"Anything new on the arson case?"

He eased into a kitchen chair and Myles glanced up. "Officer Rocco! You're home." The boy raced over and jumped into his lap. Rocco's arms went around him and he rustled his hair.

"Hey, Tiger. What have you been up to today?"

His day's activities spilled out like a swarm of butterflies flitting into the air but Rocco hung on every word, nodding emphatically and grinning then asking questions about how he built a pillow fort in Laurie's living room. How high were the pillows? Was it dark inside? Did he have a flashlight? Did he catch the bad guys when he'd played cops and robbers?

Myles had an answer for them all. It was sweet watching how they engaged, how patient Rocco was with her son. And it scared her to see the attachment Myles had for Rocco. The way he looked at him in awe and wonder—like Rocco was a real-life hero. And he was. Rocco had saved them both.

Finally, Myles hopped off his lap and returned to the trains, Dolly at his side and Cocoa next to Rocco. "That is the coolest kid." Rocco stood and went into the laundry room and scooped kibble into a bowl for Cocoa. The chocolate Lab sat patiently waiting and began to wolf down his supper only after Rocco said, "Okay."

Rocco returned to the table. "Faith things, huh?" he asked.

"Private thoughts," Sadie said and Rocco simply nodded, recognizing the hint not to pry. "Have you eaten supper?"

"No. Well, I grabbed a pack of peanut butter crackers from the vending machine. Does that count?"

"It certainly does not. Can I fix you something?"

"You certainly cannot." He grinned. "I'm a grown man who can fend for himself. I didn't ask you to stay here so you could return the favor by cooking me meals."

"I know but...you've done so much for us."

"I'm not keeping score. I feel like we've had this conversation before." He smirked and leaned forward on the table. "Sun hasn't quite set yet. How about we run through Elk Dairy and I'll grab a burger and we can get Myles a treat. Can he have a treat?"

"They have fruit pops he can have."

"Let's do that. Sit out on the picnic table and enjoy the sunset. Let's do something seminormal. It's a public place and still light out. I feel confident we'll be safe."

It would be nice to escape for a few minutes for a fruit pop. Enjoy the final days of summer as if her life wasn't in an upheaval. "All right. Sounds good." She turned toward her son. "Myles, you want a strawberry fruit pop from Elk Dairy?"

"Yay!" he hollered and looked at Dolly. "High five, Dolly." The Irish setter raised her paw and Myles gave her a high five. "Good girl. Can Dolly have one too?"

"Sure." They made safe-for-dog pops too.

After turning off the TV and grabbing her purse and Myles's backpack, they all clambered into Rocco's truck and headed for the Elk Dairy bar which was on the far side of town. A perfect place to watch the sun dip behind the mountains, leaving the sky painted in lavender and a myriad of pinks. They could watch the bison in pastures and listen to the light breeze rustle the tall field grass.

The crowd was thin except for bumping into Laurie, who

was there with John Landers from church. Sadie and Rocco eyed one another, both thinking the same thing.

A date.

After they were out of earshot, Sadie looked to Rocco. "I'm getting the scoop later." Laurie never mentioned a new man in her life, but Sadie had noticed she was in a great mood lately and she'd been wearing less messy buns and keeping her sleek blond hair styled in soft curls. John was a good guy but she understood not wanting to rock the boat and tell anyone until they knew for sure they were going to work.

"Pardon the pun," he teased.

She caught what she'd said and laughed. "Right."

Laurie lifted her phone and took a selfie with John and their ice cream treats.

"That woman lives for social media. I'm sure she's going to post it—if they work out."

"I have social media, but I rarely post unless it's of Cocoa in the backyard."

"I have zero. Laurie hounds me to open up an Instagram or TikTok or even a Snapchat just for streaks with her. Like I have time to keep a streak going."

Rocco laughed and agreed while Myles picked a picnic table near a big tree, his fruit pop already melting. The dogs licked at their doggie pops while Rocco tore into his bison burger with onion rings and Sadie enjoyed her banana and coconut fruit pop.

"Anything new about the case?" Sadie asked. "You never answered me earlier since Myles pounced."

"Isla's still running things through the ViCAP system to see if there have been any other fires using turpentine as an accelerant. We received several hits, but not all of them ended in homicide."

"Not all? So one or more did?"

"One that could have. Still processing. A guy named Rusty Remington. From Cheyenne. He was arrested after setting three fires using turpentine. One of them was a barn and the owner had been drunk and passed out. Rusty says he didn't know the man was inside. He still did time but has been out on parole for the past three months. Last known address was Laramie."

That wasn't far from here.

"I don't think I know a Rusty Remington."

"We did some digging and as it turns out, your dad knew him. Rusty worked on his construction site in Cheyenne when he was in charge of that outdoor shopping mall. It caught fire one night and your dad blamed Rusty because he'd set fires before but claimed they were accidents, not to mention he was lazy on the job. He was fired and threats were made against your father."

"You think my dad firing him has made me a target?"

"Possibly. But it seems Rusty might be a legit pyromaniac. He had no reason for burning any of those buildings. No vendettas that could be found. So I'm not sure he's our guy now. Not ruling him out, though."

"I do remember that fire. Dad talked about it, but I can't remember him mentioning it was one of his employees who might have done it. He ended up letting several men go for going back into drugs or stealing from customers. He'd been threatened before. No one ever did anything, though."

"Someone might have now."

What would harming Sadie do for him? Dad had passed. Killing her wouldn't hurt him. "I don't understand why he'd want to kill me? That's one serious grudge."

"Well, it might not be a grudge—or at least not his grudge."

"What do you mean?" Her heart stuttered. More bad news was coming. She recognized that look in his dark eyes.

"Rusty worked a painting job in Laramie and one of the other employees on the job was your ex."

It didn't take a rocket scientist to figure out where Rocco was going with the information.

"You think Hunter hired Rusty to kill us, using his grudge against my dad for firing him and the possible fact he loves fires, to convince him to do it."

"That's what I think, sadly. Hunter's parents live here. They may have told Hunter about the fires. That gave him the idea and if he knew of Rusty's fascination with watching fires burn…"

"And the other fires before mine?"

"Could be to throw us off the real target—you. Or they could be vendettas as well. Hunter's or Rusty's. We're looking into that now. Could be two separate things, like with Isla."

"That would be three separate things. More than one person taking advantage of these earlier fires. Seems a stretch." Sadie no longer had an appetite for the fruit pop. Things were becoming more tangled by the second.

No scenario ended with her and Myles alive.

Rocco put the windows down in his truck. The dogs and Myles sat in the back seat while Sadie perched next to him up front. After wiping the sticky from Myles and giving up trying to clean the sticky out of Dolly and Cocoa's fur from the fruit pop, they admired the last hints of sunset. It was twilight now, a hazy shade of gray signaling night approaching.

Rocco wanted to be home before the roads became shadowy.

Ten minutes ago, it was peaceful, beautiful and relaxing. The purple, orange, blues and pinks covered the horizon like a divine painting while Myles played and Sadie finally gave in to the normal activity. He heard it when she sighed and her shoulders visibly stood down. She'd lain back with her elbows propping her up on the picnic table top and gazed into the sky as the corners of her lips turned up. He'd like to see her this way all the time.

And he'd considered kissing her again and lingering longer than a brush of lips, but he slammed the door shut on those thoughts. He'd had no business attempting a kiss earlier, but he hadn't led with his head—he'd led with his heart, which even the Bible said was the most deceptive.

It was hard not to care about her.

She truly was a hero in his book. He turned on the radio and ran his summertime playlist through the Bluetooth. Country pop songs about boating, driving down back roads with a dog and jumping in lakes with friends belted through the speakers as the breeze filtered through their windows. Cocoa hung his head out the back window, his tongue lolling from Rocco's view in the side mirror. Cocoa loved to ride and Rocco loved having him as a best pal and cruising buddy.

The comfortable silence filled the cab of the truck and he glanced in his rearview as lights shone behind him. His stomach clenched and Sadie gripped the door with a white-knuckled grasp. Myles had closed his eyes and his hand rested on Dolly.

The car gained on him and he prayed this wouldn't happen again. They hadn't been followed. No way. How would anyone know they were here and, on this road, back to home?

The only people they'd seen were Laurie and John. Laurie had been posting photos and selfies. What if they'd been in the background of one she'd posted on several social media sites?

The killer could have seen it if he was friends with Laurie—a local no one would suspect—or if she kept her photos on "public" they would be accessible to anyone looking.

Edging up, the car then switched into the left lane and zipped past them, the driver tossing him an ugly expression. Rocco had been going the speed limit. That was unwarranted behavior but road rage was a real thing. He'd had to break up fights over it before.

Sadie released a heavy breath. "I was worried."

Same. "I think we're allowed to be on edge. And the sun's down. I was hoping to make it back before. Pitch-black night increases the creep factor by twenty."

"I hate that I'm in a situation where I have to be on edge and you're right."

"I hate you're in the situation too. I really do." He was working around the clock trying to free her from the danger. And it appeared they had a new lead. They only had to chase it down.

Out of nowhere, the truck lurched forward. Sadie yelped and Myles called through a sleepy voice, "Mommy!"

"It's okay, babe. Just hold on. We're having car trouble again."

He'd seen no lights.

Because the vehicle ramming them hadn't turned them on. He must have been behind the car that passed them. "Hold on."

The vehicle rammed into the back of him again, and he heard the pop. The tire blew and they skidded across the road, landing in the shallow ditch.

"What happened, Mommy?" Myles asked.

Rocco glanced behind them, seeing a looming shadow on the road. The truck stopped. "Hey, Tiger. Climb up here with me, okay? Quickly now. Fast like Spiderman."

Myles jumped over the seat and into Rocco's arms.

"Sadie, scoot out on my side. The truck isn't gone." He didn't want to relay too much detail. Myles was already scared, his little arms wrapped tightly around Rocco's neck.

Sadie grabbed Myles's bag and scrambled across the seat and out beside Rocco, her face pale.

"Come on Cocoa. Come, Dolly." The dogs bounded out as a bullet slammed into the side of his passenger-side door. "Head for the woods!"

Rocco ushered Sadie in front of him and Dolly and Cocoa flanked him as they ran across the ditch and climbed the fence into the pasture of bison. He didn't see any red dogs, which meant there might not be mamas ready to rumble if they approached. Bison could be aggressive and were unpredictable. Two thousand pounds that could run up to thirty-five miles an hour and horns that would gore them easily if they didn't trample them.

They might have a better shot with the gunman.

Why couldn't they have landed in the ditch of a cattle farm?

Another shot fired and the bison snorted and growled, stirring from being unsettled by the shots.

"We can't run through this pasture. It's dangerous!" Sadie cried.

"I know." But he didn't see any other option. They couldn't turn on cell phone lights for fear of giving away their position, so calling or texting for backup was a no go. And they couldn't run blindly or they might run smack into a bison. Neither of the dogs were herding dogs. "Let's crouch low and follow the fencing." The high grass would hide them and they wouldn't be in the middle of the grazing land.

A huge spotlight shone into the night and Rocco spotted several bison nearby. Not as near as they sounded, but close enough to charge if they wanted to.

"Freeze," Rocco whispered. "Down. Down." Both dogs lay still and Sadie lay flush. Rocco covered Myles. "Don't be afraid. It's like playing hide-and-seek and we're going to win. Just be real quiet, okay?"

Myles nodded and gripped Rocco's neck even tighter. He could barely breathe but he said nothing. The boy needed to feel safe and if nearly choking Rocco meant he felt secure then he'd deal with it.

The bright spotlight fanned across the fence line and Rocco prayed they were hidden enough not to be seen. He swallowed hard and clasped Sadie's hand in hopes of comforting her. His pulse raced and sweat slicked down his temples. He slipped the gun from his ankle holster, prepared to defend them to the death if necessary, but he'd rather not fire into the night for fear he'd miss and give away their position, thereby putting Sadie, Myles and the dogs in more danger than by staying silent.

The heavy footsteps of a bison rustled the grass and clomped closer to them. Probably out of curiosity, but Rocco would rather it kept its distance.

Clomp. Clomp. Clomp.

The light shone right on the bison moving toward them. He was only about ten feet away, maybe closer. If the gunman continued to follow its movements, his light would shine right on them. If Rocco fired, it would spook the beast and they could be trampled. They had no good choice to make here. Only prayer for protection, which was more important than his gun or even hiding. They needed God to hide them. To be a shield around them.

The light held on the bison and the animal paused and grunted then they were engulfed in darkness again as the spotlight swept the opposite direction before fading away.

The idling truck lights came to life and the sound of a door slamming shut echoed then he drove away.

"Why's he leaving? I mean, I'm glad but…"

"He wasn't going to take a chance coming into this pasture between the bison and me. He has to know I'm a cop and I carry a weapon at all times, and I believe God heard our prayers and answered us."

"Me too."

Rocco no longer heard the truck and the bison had moseyed back the way he'd come. "Let's wait a minute or two then head back to the truck."

"We have a blown tire. The shooter had to know we have no way to get out of here. He might circle back."

"I know." He used his cell phone and called 911 and gave the dispatcher their location and information. "We sit tight until they arrive."

Several minutes later, blue lights sliced through the night. He'd never loved the color of blue more. "Okay." He helped Sadie over the fence and handed Myles over then the dogs scrambled through some broken wire and he hopped over.

They were met by Jamie Watershed and several patrol officers. After getting statements, Jamie gave them a ride home. Rocco called a towing agency, which would pick up his truck tomorrow.

For now they were safe.

But Rocco wouldn't get a wink of sleep.

# ELEVEN

A safe house? Sadie didn't want to consider the possibility.

"Jamie has a cabin out in the middle of nowhere that was willed to him by a friend of the family who never had children," Rocco said. "It's not on the books and it's a good option to keep you and Myles safe until we find this guy."

"And what if it's weeks or months?" Sadie wasn't stupid. Cases took a lot longer than the one hour that crime TV shows took to solve them, and sometimes cases went legit cold. The EVPD's budget couldn't offer her that kind of time. It was not like she was a star witness in a mob case. She appreciated Rocco's sentiment to get her out and away. She too wanted that. But how would she provide for her and Myles? She was the sole breadwinner.

Rocco paced his kitchen floor while she perched at the table with a cup of coffee that was now lukewarm. After returning to Rocco's last night, it had taken over an hour to calm Myles down enough to drift off to sleep. The boy was traumatized. He wasn't safe with her anymore. If his own father was behind this, it wouldn't matter if he was in her care or someone else's—Hunter would be gunning for him anyway.

"I don't know the answer to how long. I only know that the attacks are escalating and I'm concerned for you and

Myles." He raked a hand through his thick hair and sighed then met her gaze. "I care about you, Sadie. I'm not going to deny that. I think it's obvious. We kissed one another. I'm not one to kiss around."

She smirked at his humor. "Neither am I."

"I know. I'm not saying it should have happened. It probably shouldn't have. We're not in good places. Timing is off. I get it. My point is I want to make you and Myles as safe as possible. I care about him too. He's awesome and this is the third time he's been a target—or collateral damage. How much more can he take before he shuts down?"

Sadie slumped over the table and covered her face with her hands. "I know. I know this. I'm torn. I can't be sure he's any safer away from me, with Laurie, than with me. Maybe I should sell, take the money Jack offered and go on the run— or go to that cabin Detective Watershed owns. Because the only way I can escape or go underground, off the grid, or into hiding—whatever you want to call it—is if I have the money to do it. I live paycheck to paycheck."

Rocco approached the table and pulled out a chair, turning it backward and straddling it. His hand rested on her shoulder. "I have money saved I—"

"No! You've done enough." She'd put him in danger, was staying at his home, pulling him away from work. She couldn't take another handout, and definitely not in cash form. "I can't ask you to and won't allow you to dump your savings into me."

"I think it'd be worth it," Rocco said "An investment in two people's lives. When Dad passed, I came into a pretty large inheritance. I don't voice it or anything but it's there. If you change your mind."

"I won't." Her eyes burned and filled with moisture. "I do

appreciate the sentiment, though." She touched his scruffy cheek. "You're a good man, Officer."

His lips twitched at her refusal to call him Rocco. She was hoping for that. The conversation was taking a too serious tone. He admitted to caring about her. He also admitted that the timing was terrible for them both, so there was no point becoming even more emotionally attached. Nothing was going to come from it.

"Before it's all said and done, Say, you're going to say my name and it's not going to be under duress."

She laughed. "We'll see." Her cell phone rang. Who would be calling her at six in the morning? She answered. "Oh, hey, Lynn." Lynn Bonet headed up the women's community book club.

"Sadie, first of all I'm so sorry about your house. I put a card in the mail like the idiot I am. As if you're there to check your mail."

"Well, I do have to check it." Bills and junk usually.

"Of course. Forgive me," she said. Lynn was like a greyhound. Slender and sleek with a long nose and small eyes, and fast. Not with her legs so much as her mouth. "I know you have a lot on your plate, pardon the pun, but Pucelli's literally went out of power and I'm hosting a party tonight for fifty women. I need a caterer and Twila said you're doing her wedding and your food is delicious. If I Venmo you the money could you handle it? Am I asking too much?"

Yes. She already had too much going on, but to present her food in front of more people meant more work opportunities. "What was the menu?"

"Lasagna, fettuccini alfredo with chicken, and cannoli. But if you want to change it up, I understand. We just read a book set in Italy and I thought it would be fun." It did sound fun and Sadie wished she had more time to read and join such a big women's book club. Maybe someday. If Lynn sent her the money she could get Blanca to cover the food truck today. Granted she'd have to pay her for the extra shift, but with this job she'd have the money. "I can pay you double what I was paying Pucelli's, since it's last-minute." She told her what she was paying the authentic rustic Italian restaurant in Laramie. Whoa. Lynn was sparing no expense. "It'll be held at the Elk Lodge at six thirty."

"I'll be happy to do it. I need to make a few phone calls and I'll get started." She also needed an industrial-sized kitchen. She glanced at Rocco and gave Lynn her Venmo username then hung up and briefed Rocco.

"I have double ovens if you want to do it here," he said.

"I'm going to call the lodge and see if I can use their kitchen. Cooking on-site would be less of a headache. I haven't purchased much for the catering business like carrying warmers."

"What's the menu?"

She relayed it and he grinned. "You have to let me help. You can't do it all by yourself. I have paid time off. I'll call in today, and I can still help Jamie if something comes up. I'll do the shopping so you can work the lunch shift and we can meet at two."

"I feel like I'm using you as a crutch."

"Think of it more like a cane. You're just leaning on me for some strength. A crutch sounds toxic and like you might be a stage-five clinger." He chuckled and she grinned.

"I'll send you money for the shopping trip. Apple or Venmo?"

"Either." He gave her his account usernames, called in a day off with the chief and Chase, and sat at the table while they compiled a list. The smell of freshly baked bread for the food truck sandwiches wafted all yeasty and scrumptious through the house with hints of coffee. Once the list was agreed on, Rocco pocketed it.

"I need to wake Myles and get him ready for the day." After waking him up and getting him dressed and fed, she dropped him at Laurie's and asked if he could spend the night since she had the book club gig. Myles had been in danger but always when Sadie was around. She was the intended target, but the killer had no problem hurting a child or anyone or pets even as collateral damage.

Could that be Hunter?

Could he have hired Rusty Remington to take out Sadie using his grudge against her late father? That was far-fetched too.

After leaving Laurie's she parked her truck in her usual spot on Main Street and rolled up the customer window. The morning was unusually cool and breezy, the air filtering through her small truck kitchen. She turned on her morning playlist, which consisted of her favorite inspirational artists, and went to work preparing for the lunch crowd. She'd considered doing breakfast as well in the future, when Myles started school. People loved hearty breakfast sandwiches and burritos, but she knew what would stretch her thin and so it was a dream for now.

She might need to sell.

She'd been praying about it but didn't feel good about selling to Jack. His personality was a huge roadblock. He was icky in every way. The street was quiet and she poked her head outside the window. Bobby Linton was coming out of the florist shop with a bouquet of flowers. Nice. She wanted him to find someone. She waved as he caught her eye, but he didn't wave back with his hands full of flowers.

A prickly sensation rose on her arms and neck and she craned her neck toward the opposite side of the florist, where

Ben Armstrong sat idling in his dark pickup. Someone was inside with him but she couldn't make out a face with the sun glaring on the windshield.

"You open for business yet?" A deep voice drew her away from the truck and the mystery passenger beside Ben. She didn't recognize the man standing at the truck's window. He was around her age, with thick chestnut hair that hung in waves past his chin. He'd tucked his bangs behind his ears and his coppery beard gave him a gruff appearance but his dark eyes seemed kind.

"Oh, no, I don't serve breakfast. Lunch and dinner. Sorry."

"I followed my nose. Smells good."

She smiled. "Thank you. I don't suppose you're from around here."

"Nah," he said and jammed his hands in his faded denim pockets. "I've been here before but I'm only passing through. I'm known to get sidetracked."

Sadie nodded. She could relate. "Well, we'll open at eleven if you're around."

"I may have to swing back through. What's the best item on the menu?"

"The meatball sub," she answered and thought of Rocco, who would disagree aloud but the fact he ordered it on the daily said otherwise.

"Nice. I like a good sub." He glanced at the side of the truck. "Sadie. I'm assuming you're Sadie."

"I am. And you are?"

He offered a hand. "Rusty. Rusty Remington."

Sadie's throat turned to cotton and she swallowed hard. "You worked for my dad."

He frowned. "You Sadie Owens?"

He'd been in prison for setting three fires and one man

had died. And he was right here in front of her face and food truck. "I think you know exactly who I am."

Rusty cocked his head. "Why should I know that? Look, whatever your dad may have said about me isn't true. You got that scared-cat look in your eye."

A car pulled to the curb and Sadie let out a breath of relief. Rocco.

"Rusty Remington. I've been looking for you. I believe you received a call from Detective Jamie Watershed to come on in and have a chat. Seems we've been having some fires around town and isn't it interesting that here you are…a known fire bug."

Rusty glared at Rocco and then glanced at Cocoa as if weighing the idea of starting something. Cocoa would protect Rocco if he needed it, but Sadie was certain Rocco could take care of himself.

"Well, Officer, it's a free country and I was just inquiring about some grub. No crime there. And I did talk to that detective earlier this morning. In fact, that's where I just been. I'll tell you—" he turned to Sadie "—and you, what I told him. I didn't kill nobody or set any fires in this town. And I did my time for the ones I did set. I have alibis for the recent fires. He's checking them now, and they'll come back solid. As for your daddy," he said to Sadie, "he fired me for something he couldn't prove I did."

"Either way," Rocco said. "You leave Sadie alone and steer clear of her place of business."

"Free country, dude. I can go anywhere I please, unless you put a restraining order against me. You got one of those?"

Rocco sniffed and made himself a barrier between the food truck and Rusty. "I know you're on parole. If I dig hard enough, I'll find you've broken it. Won't I? You want to go back to prison? Walk away."

Rusty spat on the ground. "Good day," he added with a snarl and stalked down the street. When Sadie glanced up, Ben was watching from his truck but whoever had been in the passenger side was gone.

Rocco hadn't been able to concentrate most of the day since Rusty's display at the food truck. Had he been telling the truth about not realizing Sadie's father owned that food truck and gave it to her? Possibly. Six years ago, she was running it while her father ran the construction business full-time, but it didn't sit right with him.

Jamie corroborated Rusty's story. The ex-con had been at the precinct earlier this morning to answer endless questions. Jamie had made a call to someone he knew in Texas who was now a private consultant and she'd mentioned that if Rusty hadn't set any other fires, but he might have and simply not been caught, he was unlikely to be a pyromaniac. Pyros couldn't help themselves. They had a deep-seated need to burn things. But being in town upped him on their suspect list.

Now Rocco was parked outside the Elk Valley Lodge. He'd done the shopping for Sadie and unloaded the groceries earlier. He'd had time to spare, so he'd chopped some vegetables too. Cooking helped him think and he had a lot on his mind.

Hunter had a lot to lose if Sadie hauled him into court for back child support. He was in town, was a known trouble-maker and had a connection with Rusty Remington, having worked with him in Laramie for a painting crew. It was possible Hunter had paid or bartered crimes, like that movie where strangers on a train murdered each other's foes.

What would Rusty want from Hunter? If that was even the case.

Hunter had played baseball under coach Ed Towers. Rocco didn't remember hearing any rumors of bad blood between them. And how did Herman Willows fit in?

Jack Norwood wanted her food truck and, quite frankly, he wanted Sadie out of the market so he could cash in. He wanted property from Herman Willows and Coach Towers. He'd also allegedly burned down his restaurant for the insurance money, though it couldn't be proved, and they had paid out, which had bought him two food trucks and a stellar new kitchen, from what he'd heard around town.

If Elk Valley did anything, it was talk. Rumors had hurt people. It was rumored that Trevor Gage invited Naomi Carr-Cavanaugh to the Young Rancher's Club dance ten years ago in order to prank her and humiliate her.

It had worked.

Her brother Evan Carr could be the RMK, retaliating on her behalf.

Or Ryan York could have avenged his sister Shelly's death, if he was the RMK.

Of course, the RMK case had nothing to do with the arson/murder case but both had been driving him up a wall. Then again, he'd considered the fact that the RMK might be behind all the trouble to throw off the task force from catching him. That seemed unlikely, though, since the RMK's MO was well established. Rocco's mind batted both cases back and forth like a ping-pong ball.

Sadie pulled up at two on the nose and climbed out of her car and waved. "You been waiting for me long?"

"Nah. Chief Quan told me to keep my patrol vehicle just in case but said a day of PTO would do me good." It hadn't, though. He was still working the case.

"Nice. The dinner shift is covered. Blanca is handling it."

Rocco walked her into the big rustic lodge. The place

looked like a hunting ground with myriads of elk, deer and bison heads hanging on walls and a massive bear head hanging over the mantel. The walls were cedar and open beams with big rustic chandeliers created nice lighting. It smelled like raw cedar, pine and money. Mostly the elite met here. "Lynn must run a bougie book club."

"You think?" Sadie teased and strode down the hallway to the kitchen in the back of the lodge.

Rocco explained he'd chopped the veggies and where he'd put everything.

"You didn't have to do all that extra work, but thanks. My feet are killing me. I need new shoes. My poor ones are worn out. Between being on them all day and chasing my kid around, the tread doesn't last long."

"I hear ya. That kid is full of energy. Reminds me of me when I was his age," he said as he washed his hands and grabbed a white apron from the stainless steel counter. "I'm sous-chef so give me an order."

"Oh, bossing you around is going to be a real treat." She winked and his stomach dipped before going airborne like when he'd gone joyriding with friends and jumped train tracks.

"Boss away," he flirted and held her gaze.

"Then get to making the filling for the lasagna."

"Aye, aye."

The next two hours they worked together like old pros who'd been in business for ages, while making small talk and purposely avoiding case talk. They needed the break. He stirred the sauce he'd had simmering the past hour and held up a tasting spoon. "What do you think?" he held out the spoon and she blew on it then tasted.

His stomach jumped the tracks again. Cooking with her, tasting food together felt intimate.

"That's amazing. Not even gonna lie," he said. "Have you tasted it yet or am I the guinea pig?"

A dot of marinara colored her bottom lip and he leaned in. "I haven't. Maybe I should." He studied her and waited a beat to be stalled out but she didn't move. Didn't look away.

"Maybe so."

He took his cue and lightly brushed his lips over hers. "It's good," he murmured, cradling her cheek, enjoying her nearness with wonder and amazement.

His hand slid to her jaw and her slender arms slipped around his neck, her fingertips in his hair. Suddenly she froze and pulled back. "Do you smell that?"

He sniffed. "The meatballs!" He rushed to the oven, grabbed an oven mitt and pulled out the pan of meatballs he'd been baking.

"Are they burnt?" she asked.

"We saved them but it was a close call." And they probably needed a distraction. Not that Rocco would have pulled her close and made out or anything, but while he couldn't speak for her, his emotions were becoming ridiculously tangled. The longer he kissed her, the more they twisted and turned and revealed how deep they might go.

Thoughts of his dad being preoccupied and not being around for Mom in those last days sprang up. He couldn't do that to Sadie. Or anyone. He had to solve these cases before he could let himself fall for someone. His work had to be a priority. He owed his dad. He owed the town and wanted to bring healing to the community.

And now he had Sadie's case that needed his undivided attention.

"We could have burned the place down and *you* might end up on the suspect list," Sadie said and fanned the smoke coming from the oven. Grease had dripped into the bottom, causing the burning smell, and the place reeked of smoke.

"Ha ha. But I'm glad you can be funny about it."

"If they'd burned I might cry. I don't have time to make new ones."

He grinned. "I might too." He paused. "So about that kiss…are we good? Is it going to be weird?"

"You're weird, so yeah," she teased. "No, it won't be weird but it also can't happen again although I feel like we've already said that. Timing and all. You have your job and it's a big one and Myles is a lot of work and his diabetes might be permanent. I have no plans to saddle that load on you—"

"Yoo-hoo! Sadie." Lynn's voice broke through the conversation and she popped her head into the kitchen. "It smells divine in here minus the smoke and burned scent. What happened? Is our dinner ruined?"

Rocco only half listened. Had Sadie just dumped him in the rotten men category with her ex? Saddling Myles on him? Myles wasn't a load he had to carry that would be burdensome. He wasn't scared off by the diabetes or anything else. Did she truly think he would be or was she projecting?

Either way, he couldn't deny it felt like he'd been bitten by fire ants on a hot July day. He needed to revisit this conversation but now was clearly not the time. Lynn was already sampling meatballs and listening to Sadie explain the grease dripping on the bottom of the stove.

His phone buzzed.

Text from Isla.

I have news. Could potentially be big in the arson case.

# TWELVE

"I wish I could go with you," Sadie said to Rocco. "You'll call me as soon as you know anything, won't you?"

Rocco laid a hand on her shoulder. "I promise." Lynn had left them in the kitchen to work on the table centerpieces, and now was not the time to bring up the issue with him bolting on her son Myles because he was a burden. "Go kill it out there."

Sadie grinned. "Poor choice of words."

Man, she kept a perpetual smile on his face.

"If I don't hear from you I'll see you at the house."

His stomach pulled at that comment. As if they shared a home. Their home. "Okay. Have someone walk you out and be careful. If no one is available call me and I'll escort you. Better safe than sorry."

She nodded. "You better go and I need to serve the food while it's hot."

He squeezed her shoulder then headed to his car and drove to the Elk Valley PD.

Isla's office was on the first floor and when he entered, she was sitting at her desk, her hair piled on her head as she pored over notes. She glanced up. "Hey, Rocco. Come in. Have a seat."

"What do you have?"

"Detective Watershed mentioned Jack Norwood as a person of interest. Jack's a big bison in a little pasture here and he's best friends with Willard Chambers."

"Lee Chambers's father."

"Right. They were business partners in some big real estate development throughout Wyoming and even Montana. I did some digging with Jamie's approval. Turns out that Lee Chambers made a visit on behalf of Jack Norwood to Herman Willows about six months before he died in the fire, and he also has contacted Coach Towers's family about selling, which you already know. I wondered if he might have talked to Ed Towers about selling *prior* to his death."

Rocco's pulse spiked. "He did?"

"Yes. According to Towers's son, Ed called and told him that Lee had come by to talk to him about selling to Jack. The kids wanted him to and for a great price, but Ed wasn't ready and declined."

Rocco rubbed his chin as this new information sent his mind spinning. "Jack wants Sadie's business. She never mentioned him sending Lee to talk to her, but she might have. Do you think Lee Chambers did Jack Norwood's dirty work?"

"I think it's reasonable to believe but circumstantial."

Would this be enough for a judge to give him a warrant to search phone records and Lee or Jack's home for turpentine? Probably not. "Jamie mention interviewing Lee?"

"No, but I imagine he will. He'll probably call you to sit in or even conduct the interview. You go back to high school days with Lee."

He had rapport even though he'd never cared for Lee or his crowd of egotistical, privileged meatheads. "I'll call Jamie. Thanks, Isla. This is good stuff." He stood. "Any news on little Enzo?"

"My house is being repaired so it's not out of the realm of possibility. I'd love to know who's trying to ruin my life and sabotage any hopes of me becoming a foster mom. Granny Annie says to keep on trusting God even in the darkest of times. I'm trying."

"I hear ya." When Dad had passed it had been a tough time leaning into God. He'd had so many questions and hurt feelings. "We'll find out who's after you. And if you need to stay with me again, let me know." He doubted it was necessary, though. They'd ruled it a copycat and didn't suspect the fire had been set to kill Isla but to kill her chances of fostering to adopt by depriving her of a home.

"Thanks. I'm staying with Granny Annie now and I think we'll be okay."

"Call if you need anything."

After leaving her office, he headed for Jamie's. Jamie glanced up and waved him over. "I was about to call you. I've got some news."

"Isla filled me in. I just came from her office."

"Good. She mention I want you to do the interview? I know you're not a detective but I think you'll have more rapport with him."

Rocco released a heavy breath. "I'm happy to do it, but Lee isn't exactly a friend of mine. He wasn't super cooperative in my reinterviewing for the young ranchers' murders but I'll give it my best. Play the Elk Valley hometown boys card. See where it lands. Have you called him?"

"I have. Told him I needed some help in connecting a few dots in the case. He doesn't suspect we are looking at him for the crimes. Made him more helpful and he should be here within twenty minutes. Can you stick around?"

"Yeah, I'm technically off today. Took some PTO to help out Sadie."

He grinned. "Going above and beyond on this case, Officer."

Rocco shook his head. "I won't lie and say I don't care about her. I do. But—"

"Don't let big buts get in the way. And I already know what you're going to say. You're too entangled in the job. It's your first priority. From bringing this community back together to making your father proud. Can I tell you what will make your father proud? Having a life. Falling in love. Giving your mom grandkids."

Jamie had him pegged big-time.

"When you're old and gray and too feeble to be a cop, you won't look back and regret all the cases you didn't solve—though you'll wish you had. No, you'll have wished to be more present in the lives of those you love. Those will be your biggest regrets. I know. I'm divorced for a reason, Rocco. Nobody cheated. Nobody lied. Nobody stopped loving each other. My job was my first love and Elena grew tired of not being in the spot she should have. I was too stupid to make changes. Too stubborn to put my job in its rightful place. Justice was important. Lives being saved was what mattered and nothing saved my marriage. I let it fall apart. And when I did come to the realization that I'd been wrong it was too late and Elena was already remarried and pregnant with the family she'd wanted with me."

Rocco felt the punch to his gut.

Jamie's intercom buzzed and the admin assistant let him know Lee Chambers was in the interview room.

"Just think about what I said," Jamie said as they walked down the hall to the room. "Now, onto the case. We need Lee to offer up alibis for the nights of the fires and to admit he'd talked to Ed Towers and Herman Willows about selling their land to Jack Norwood."

Rocco nodded and entered the interview room with Cocoa where Lee Chambers sat like he was here to hang out with bros. Chambers's dad was powerful and Lee believed he was untouchable. If Rocco came in combative, it would shut Lee up and their investigation down. He needed to tread lightly. "Lee," he said and shook his hand, registering the surprise on Lee's face at seeing a patrol officer here to talk instead of the detective. He could see it two ways. One, he wasn't in any trouble, or two, he was insulted.

"How you doing, man? This won't take long." Rocco rolled his eyes. "Just need some help."

"Cool. Cool." Lee's shoulders relaxed. "I thought this was about the fires, not the RMK case."

"Oh, it is. I'm helping Jamie with that since I have the arson dog."

Lee glanced at his chocolate Lab and grinned. "Crazy what dogs can sniff out."

"You're telling me." Rocco changed the subject. "How's your mom doing?"

"She's on a new med for the Parkinson's but hasn't been on it long enough to know if it will help or not. Thanks for asking," he said with a softer voice. Lee might be a tool but he loved his mom and everyone knew it. It was the way to soften him and Rocco hated that she had this disease. She'd always been active in the community until lately.

"I hope it works for her. I really do."

"Thanks. Me too. Your mom came by not too long ago and brought a pie. Real nice of her. Thank her for me, will you?"

"I will." Time to get to it and the best way was to keep Lee in the dark. "I have some questions about Jack Norwood."

His dark eyes widened. "Jack? Jack didn't set any fires, Rocco. You know this."

"Well, I tend to agree but we do know that Jack inquired about Coach's and Herman Willows's properties and he also has approached Sadie Owens in regards to buying out Sadie's

Subs and the recipes. They all turned him down and not long after that two out of three died in a house fire. Sadie and her son barely escaped the one at her house. And someone is still gunning for Sadie. We also know that after Ed and Herman's death, Jack reached out about the sale again and it looks like he's going to get what he wants."

Lee frowned. "That doesn't make Jack a killer."

"No, but it does look shady, dude. I mean you have to admit that. I don't think a jury would find it unreasonable to believe, especially when Jack's own business was burned down and while they leaned accidental it was inconclusive." He splayed his hands. "I'm not saying he did any of it. I'm just saying it doesn't look good for him."

Lee studied Rocco's face then nodded.

"I told Jamie I wanted to talk to you because…" Rocco leaned in as if about to reveal a deep secret. "I know you work for Jack and your dad. And I know Jack sent you to inquire about the sales, minus Sadie. I personally wanted to talk to you first, before questioning Jack, which we will. To protect you."

He flinched. "Protect me from what?"

"Jack. If he knows he's in trouble, and he also knows you've inquired about the land for him, guess who he'll throw under the bus first chance he gets to save his own bacon?"

Lee pointed to his chest. "I didn't burn any house to the ground or kill anyone."

"I know. That's why I have you here. I wanted to get my ducks in a row before dealing with slick Jack. If you have rock-solid alibis for those murders and the attempted murder on Sadie and her son, Jack can't win. I'll be able to tell him that making you the fall guy isn't going to work."

"Jack would never do that. He's a jerk, but he's not a killer."

"And yet he had you do the initial asking. If he did do it, he can blame you. Do you want to risk being arrested, going to trial and possibly prison because you think he didn't do it?"

Lee's jaw worked and he sighed. "The night Sadie's house burned down I was at the batting cages with friends."

Rocco slid a notepad and pen across the table. "Write their names and numbers down. You're doing yourself a favor here. Also, how'd you bat?" Keep it cordial. Easy. Relaxed.

"You don't want to know. It was terrible." He half chuckled and began writing.

"What about the night Ed Towers died?" He reminded him of that July night.

"Softball until seven then out with my girlfriend, Andrea. Home around midnight."

That didn't give him an alibi for the time of Ed's death. Either Lee was innocent or stupid for not giving an alibi to match the time frame of the fire. "By yourself?"

Lee grinned. "No. She was with me all night. Left around seven Sunday morning. Works the brunch shift at Elk Valley Café."

"Put her number down too. This is a huge favor to us." Stroke his ego. Make him feel important.

"As for Herman Willows, that was a week night. I was probably home alone. I don't usually go out much during the week. I know that doesn't look good but it's the truth." He shrugged. He could have lied. Any one of his friends would commit perjury for Lee. Maybe he was telling the truth.

Or he was that good.

"And as for Sadie Owens…"

Lee shifted uncomfortably in his chair and rubbed his hands on his thighs. The whole atmosphere tilted at her name. Why?

"I never approached Sadie about selling. But Jack's wanted her business forever. In his eyes, she's his biggest threat. She takes his lunch and dinner crowd away habitually. People would rather stand in line and eat on the curb from her than sit inside at his fine establishment. My father encouraged him to purchase a couple of food trucks himself. 'It's the thing these days with the young people,' according to Pops."

Jack did purchase two of them. After his restaurant burned down and he obtained the insurance money. "That didn't really work for him, though, did it?"

"No. They're hemorrhaging money but he thought if Sadie sold the business and recipes he could paint them like hers and make three Sadie's Subs and do some traveling with one of them. Lot of RV events and campgrounds to gain business. She's balking, though. I mean, I get it. Her dad gave her that business and it's all that's left. Still…she's hard up for money and she'd make a killing to start a new business. A new food truck even."

"Not without her original recipes, though, and those are what sell like hotcakes."

"Exactly. Jack knows this. And what Jack wants he eventually gets. We all know that too." Lee leaned back and studied his alibis then slid the notebook back over. "I don't think he'd resort to murder but I'm not going down for him."

"No, you will not." Rocco shook his hand again and waved him off. When he was gone, Jamie entered the room.

"He didn't give you a single solid alibi. He could have sneaked out when his girlfriend was asleep, or like Evan Carr's girlfriend, Paulina—she could lie for him. Nothing is concrete. He could be playing right along with us. He's believable. Has just too much confidence to be worried. You did a great job, by the way."

"Thanks. Played the friend card."

"Well played. Do you think he did it?" Jamie asked.

"I don't know." Rocco's radio buzzed and the information splashed over his heart like ice water.

A fire had broken out at the Elk Valley Lodge.

Sadie.

Sadie pushed on the kitchen door leading to the dining area but someone had barricaded it. After dinner, she'd popped in her earbuds to listen to Christi Cold's true crime podcast, *Dead Talk*, and hadn't heard anything. By the time she'd scrubbed the pans and loaded up, she couldn't get out the door or the kitchen door leading to the parking lot. Someone had either locked her in or barricaded it too.

That was when she began to smell the smoke and see it slithering in through the bottom of the door, in snakelike ribbons.

She called 911 from her cell phone but she wasn't sure how much time she had.

Smoke now poured in from both doors and overhead, as if someone had sneaked into the ductwork and set it ablaze. Fire was licking the door leading to the interior of the lodge and was beginning to eat along the ceiling.

Dropping to the floor, she snatched a dish towel and covered her mouth and nose. She coughed as the smoke entered her lungs, causing irritation. The heat alone was nearly unbearable. Sweat trailed down her temples and back and her eyes burned and watered.

She wasn't sure how long ago she'd made the 911 call. Probably only seconds but it felt like hours. Like she was going to be consumed in these malicious flames, flicking their tongues in anticipation of devouring her whole.

Thoughts bulleted through her mind. She had no will for Myles. Who would take him? Hunter? No way. He wouldn't want him unless it gave him access to insurance money and anything he might inherit, like the family home and property and the food truck. His parents? They never even tried to see him and were only fifteen minutes away. The foster care system? She'd heard too many nightmares about how some children were mistreated, shunted from one bad home to another like cattle.

Rocco? Would Rocco take him? He'd been good to him but he didn't have time to be in a relationship. Being a father wouldn't be on his priority list. He might resent her. Isla. Yes! Isla wanted to foster and adopt. She would take good care of Myles.

But Sadie didn't want to leave her son.

She wanted God to rescue her from the burning flames taunting her. Jumping up, she turned on the faucet and shoved in the rubber stopper so it would run over and spill out onto the tile flooring. Granted, this wouldn't touch the fire licking its way across the ceiling and now one of the walls across from her. Eating, eating, eating. Never satisfied. Always hungry like the grave.

She crawled into the industrial sink and into the water, placing a wet towel over her head. There was no way out. No way through. Was God in the fire with her? Was He walking through the flames with her? She prayed He was.

Pieces of ceiling tile burned up and fell in black, sooty pieces all around. Popping like gunshots and hissing like serpents echoed through the kitchen. If they didn't come soon, it would be a recovery mission, not a rescue. Sadie cried and crouched in the cold water of the big industrial sink, water now spilling onto the counters and floor. She used a clear water pitcher and filled it and threw it on the walls around her. Repeating the process over and over, hoping to keep the fire at bay. Her skin was hot to the touch and she couldn't stop coughing.

Lightheadedness toppled her to the side and her stomach roiled. Nausea swept over her and her limbs grew heavy and exhausted to the point she could barely pick up the empty plastic pitcher. She finally filled it and dumped it on her head to cool herself and keep from passing out, but her strength waned.

The flames now reached above her head and hot pieces of fiberglass dropped on her skin, burning her flesh. She cried out and then heard a horrendous rumble and pop. Was the roof caving in? *God, help me!*

The door from the parking lot into the kitchen had been broken from the hinges and lay flat on the floor. Someone pushed between two firefighters.

"Don't tell me what to do!" he bellowed and then she saw.

Rocco. Rocco had come for her. Pushing past the protests and entering the burning room. He spotted her and ran, ducking as pieces of ceiling rained down. He lifted her from the sink of cold water, her jeans drenched and the wet towel draped over her head. "I've got you now," he said through a squint and cough. "Just hold on to me. Hold on."

She locked her arms around his neck as he cradled her and rushed toward the door. Firefighters were already dousing the flames. The night air felt amazing on her flushed skin and she tried to inhale the fresh air but sputtered and coughed, her chest burning. Paramedics worked on her, putting an oxygen mask on her face.

"Did you see anyone?" Rocco asked, pushing away paramedics. "I'm fine," he snapped. Soot covered his scruffy, handsome face and ash rested in his dark hair. The guy raised his hands and backed off.

"Your lungs sound clear but I think you should seek further care at the hospital. But it's your choice," the blond-haired man said.

Sadie pulled the mask off. "I didn't see anyone or hear anything. I—I don't want to go to the hospital." One more bill she didn't need and who knew what the transport alone would cost.

"Are you sure?" Rocco lifted her chin and studied her. "If you had millions of dollars would you go?"

Maybe. Probably.

"How long was I in there?"

"From the call to 911 until I carried you out was four minutes and twenty-six seconds." He held her gaze and her eyes filled with tears.

"You were…you counted down the minutes."

"Down to every terrifying second I didn't know you were safe."

She reached up and touched his filthy cheek, his whiskers tickling her fingertips. "Rocco," she said through a raspy breath. That was all that would push from her lips. She had no words to convey how much it meant to her. How much he meant to her.

"Duress. I want to hear my name when you're not under it. But I'll take it. For now." He used the pad of his thumb to wipe her tears trickling down her hot cheeks.

The EMT released her after she signed the form stating she didn't want extra medical treatment.

"Let me drive you home, okay?"

She wasn't going to argue. She'd stored extra food in a cooler in her car and Rocco loaded it up while she waited in the passenger seat of his truck, which looked like it had been fixed at some point today. The bumper and side door were no longer smooshed.

She buckled up but even a seat belt wouldn't hold back her shivers. This fire had been too close. Near fatal. She called Laurie and asked if she could talk to Myles if he wasn't already asleep. She wanted to hear his voice. Tell him good-night. But he was already fast asleep and safe. Probably better that way. He might pick up on her flustered tone. She was more than flustered.

She was terrified.

Rocco climbed inside and took her hand. "How you holding up? Be honest."

"I'm not. I don't think I've ever been so scared and all I could think about was what would happen to my son if something happened to me." Her voice broke on the last thought and she bent forward, placing her face in her hands as sobs erupted.

Rocco's strong arm came around her side. He didn't say a word but he let her lean into him and let it all out, which was exactly what she needed at this moment. No words. Just all her fear and uncertainty and confusion spilled out through tears. While he was solid in muscle, he was a soft place for her to land.

A safe place.

But for how long?

# THIRTEEN

Rocco sat in Luna's kitchen, inhaling the scent of cinnamon and vanilla as she prepared French toast for him, Sadie and Myles. It was now Saturday morning. A week had passed since Sadie's home had been set on fire, and this most recent Friday night's fire had turned to ash, but it still blazed hot inside Rocco—and inside Sadie's chest, if he had to guess.

When he'd heard the call, it had sent him over the edge. He'd tossed out all reason and logic and barreled into the lodge, not caring if he was burned or injured. All he could think about was Sadie and a world without her. Unimaginable.

She'd been smart under the gun, though. Crawling into a huge sink of water and putting a wet towel over her head to keep her as safe as possible until help could come. The woman was resilient but the days and attacks were taking their toll. She sat at the other end of the table, elbows on the old wooden top, with a steaming cup of Italian roast that Luna had shipped in from Italy. Luna was a coffee snob but he didn't mind, since he benefited.

Myles played trains on Luna's coffee table. She glanced up every now and then and watched him, amusement dancing in her dark eyes. If she started in on the "when was she going to see great-grandchildren" while they ate brunch, he'd crawl in a hole and die.

He was going to have to deal with these feelings. If only he knew how.

"Rocco tells me you make a meatball sub," Luna said to Sadie.

Sadie gave him a look then smiled at his Luna. "I do."

Luna leaned in and laid a wrinkled but strong hand on her shoulder. "Don't let him convince you it needs more basil. He overdoes it on the basil. Thinks it's salt, I tell you."

Sadie laughed. "I'll have you know I agree wholeheartedly. I've been telling him it's my bestseller and to leave it alone."

Luna laughed and winked at Rocco. "I like her. And I'd love to try one of those subs. I don't get out much these days. Arthritis and sciatica. But I could manage to get out for one of those."

"I'll do better than that," Sadie said. "I'll bring you one straight to your front door and even sit with you while you enjoy it. Because rest assured, Ms. Manelli, you will love it."

"Confidence is good. I look forward to it." She slid the baking dish of French toast into the oven and Rocco could already taste the real maple syrup and butter slathered on the thick slabs of Texas toast.

His phone dinged and it was a text from the task force leader Chase Rawlston. Video call at noon. Something big must be going down or they caught a break in the RMK case. Maybe Isla found which boutique the killer had purchased the KILLER collar for Cowgirl from and they could track him.

Evan Carr. Ryan York. None of the above.

Tall and blond wasn't a lot to go on. He'd feel better once they could interview Evan again and locate and interview Ryan again. He texted back that he'd be there.

"Everything okay?" Sadie asked.

"Yeah. Work never ends. Video meeting today at noon." He set a reminder on his phone in case time slipped away. The days were unpredictable lately. Anything could happen. Jamie's offer for the secluded cabin was still on the table. He didn't want to leave her and Myles there alone and he didn't have much PTO to spend. This was definitely worth it, though. And it was August. He'd get two more weeks in January.

Now wasn't the time to discuss it.

Instead they sat around the table with a second pot of coffee, talking about Luna growing up in Italy and visiting in summers, gardening, faith, children and a million other things. The conversation flowed freely and was sprinkled with laughter until the timer dinged and Luna pulled the French toast from the oven.

"It smells wonderful. I've been toying with doing a brunch once a month to start on Saturday mornings. I'd love this recipe."

"You are welcome to it," Luna said.

"Myles, come wash your hands." Myles trotted over with Dolly beside him. Sadie held him up over the sink and washed his chubby little hands then placed him at the table on a stack of books. Dolly lay at his feet next to Cocoa, who was under the table snoozing.

Luna asked Rocco to say the blessing and he bowed and prayed over the food and for protection and peace and wisdom.

Sadie drenched her breakfast in butter and syrup and took a bite, making a major to-do over it. "This is incredible. I definitely could use this recipe."

Myles ate a big bite, syrup dripping down his chin in a sticky trail. "I like pancakes."

"French toast, baby. It's like pancakes but a little different."

He nodded. "I like it."

"Me too," Rocco added.

They ate in relative silence and Sadie helped Luna clean up and wash dishes while Rocco and Myles went out back to the tire swing his grandfather had made for him when he was about Myles's age. He helped the boy inside the tire and gave him a push while Dolly stayed nearby and Cocoa sniffed around a tree.

"I like to swing, Officer Rocco. I have a swing set at my house but it burned all down and Mommy says we're gonna live somewhere else. I thought we lived in your house."

Rocco's heart fluttered. "Oh…well…you're staying with me for a little while and then your mommy will find you a new house, but guess what? You get to take your swing set. It didn't burn down."

The wind caught Myles's hair, flapping his bangs in the breeze. As the swing came backward, Myles caught Rocco's eye for a quick second. "I want us to live with you. Can we put my swing set at your house?"

*Oh boy.* How did one explain complicated relationships to a three-year-old? "I love that you like my house. You can be there anytime you want, but me and your mommy won't live together. We think only married people live together."

"You should marry her and we can stay with you."

*Oh boy times ten.* "Want me to push you higher?" he asked, hoping to derail this conversation to a more kid-friendly discussion.

"Yeah!"

"Okay. Up you go!" He gave him a big push and Myles giggled. The kid had a great laugh. He was actually the best little guy Rocco knew.

"I'm flying, Officer Rocco. Look!"

"I see you. You're flying so high. Like a big jet."

Sadie sauntered into the yard, looking gorgeous in a plain white T-shirt and faded jeans. Nothing special but she didn't need anything to make her any more special than she already was. "We got it all cleaned up. Luna is going to rest her eyes, she said. I took that as a cue to nap. Thanks for bringing us. She's great."

"Look at me, Mommy. Officer Rocco says I'm a big jet."

"You are. The biggest and fastest," she added and grinned.

"Rocco says we can move the swing set. I want to move it to his house so he can marry you and we can live with him. I like living at Officer Rocco's."

Sadie's cheeks flushed. "Some days I wish I hadn't talked to him like an adult. More baby talk might mean less of a stellar vocab on him. I'm sorry," she said quietly. "I had feared this might happen." She walked in front of the swing. "Officer Rocco and I aren't getting married and we can't live with him. We're going to find us a new fun house with a backyard and we'll put your swing set there and maybe even buy us a sandbox."

"Yeah! A sandbox."

She glanced at Rocco and sighed. "If you don't mind giving us a ride to Laurie's before you have to work, that would be great. We'll hang out there the rest of the day and...then we'll find a new place to stay tonight."

Rocco's gut knotted. "It's not...safe," he whispered and slowed down the swing. "Hey, Tiger, how about you go explore the yard with the dogs. Keep them busy."

Myles saluted and called the dogs, running for the bird feeder at the back of the fence.

"You shouldn't leave. Cocoa and I can protect you. It makes the most sense." She needed to stay where he could protect her. Watch over her.

"He's found me with or without you. I have to do what is best for my son."

"Leaving me puts him in jeopardy."

"Staying does too!" she said, raising her voice. "He's attached to you. I feared that might happen and it has. It's not fair to him, and the longer we hole up in your house, the harder it will become for him. When we leave, he'll miss you and his heart will break that you're gone. He can't handle that kind of rejection and pain again."

Rocco studied her. Her bottom lip quivered and her hands were balled at her sides. He closed the distance between them. "He can't handle it—or you can't?"

Sadie sat on Laurie's couch. Laurie had finally opened up about her date with John and about how things were going well. Then she'd asked about what happened at Rocco's Luna's house this morning. So Sadie had unloaded.

"What did you say after he asked you if you were talking about you or Myles?" Laurie asked as Sadie sat on the small leather love seat with a cup of peppermint tea.

"I told him I didn't want to talk about it. He was helping me out and I appreciated it, but my emotional state and deep personal life was none of his business and we'd crossed too many lines anyway. It was time for me to leave."

Laurie flinched. "Yikes. You really unloaded on him."

Sadie had. She was angry. Not at Rocco but at herself. He'd seen what she didn't want to see. That she was the one growing attached to Rocco. She didn't want to feel the rejection and abandonment she'd felt after Hunter left, and indirectly after her father passed away.

But even more so…she was angry at God. He'd taken Dad when she needed support. He'd let her house be taken and her son be sick and her marriage to fail. The truth was also buried with her raw feelings. The truth that people died. People left. And her own choices had led to and would lead to consequences. Hunter hadn't been any good for her and her father had told her so, and yet, she'd decided to do what she wanted.

And there were things that were flat out of her control. Like someone trying to kill her.

"I'm a mess, Laurie. A hot, stinking mess."

"I hear ya," her friend said and leaned back on the couch, tucking her legs up under her while Myles and Dolly played in the dining room she'd turned into a den full of toys with a big TV and books. "We're all hot messes. I think you're scared to take a chance on another man because you've had bad experiences before and because you miss your dad. His death was a stark reality that people aren't here forever. Here today. Gone tomorrow. No one really knows when their time will be up. You're afraid of falling for Rocco for fear he'll leave you on purpose or accidentally, but either way, you don't want to take the risk, and yet you're falling for him."

Leave it to Laurie to nail it.

"I can't talk about it right now. I have Jack Norwood on my back about selling. It would be easy. Take the money. Use it for a catering business and pay off a lot of bills looming over my head. But Sadie's Subs is my dad's gift to me and to sell him the recipes means I can't ever use them again. But they're my signature dishes and people will want them. And Jack won't buy without the recipes."

Laurie frowned and then scrolled through her social media apps. "Jack Norwood isn't doing you a favor. He's trying to cut you out and make more money for himself. I mean, pray about it, but I'd tell him to pound sand. You don't need his money to pay off bills. God will make a way somehow. He's already given you a few venues and you said yourself Lynn and the book club ladies raved."

True. She'd received a text to cater an anniversary party and a business luncheon next month. She'd used her own marinara for the pasta dish and if she sold to Jack, she'd lose that. Laurie had a point. Quick fixes weren't always the best solution in the long run. And that was all Jack was, a quick fix to a problem that would return. Sadie's Subs was at least consistent work. Catering was hit or miss. Then she'd have new concerns and anxiety about acquiring gigs to make ends meet. She couldn't live on Jack's offer forever.

"Girl!" Laurie said and lurched forward, grinning and staring at her phone.

"What?"

"Why didn't you tell me you finally took the plunge?" She held up the phone and the social media app. "You got a profile. Finally. Who are you trying to reconnect with?"

Sadie stared at her face, a photo of her smiling from inside her food truck and waving. "I didn't set up a personal profile. What is that?"

"You. Your name. Live in Elk Valley. Single mom. Business owner. I can't see your friends. Why have you not friended me?" She sported a fake pout. "For real, though. It's about time you get on board. This is life now. Did you download Snapchat too? Streaks!"

"No. I didn't set up any account. Let me see that." She snatched Laurie's phone and studied her picture. "I didn't even take this photo. I have no idea who did and I did not set up this profile. I've been cloned. Is that a thing?"

"Well, yeah. That's the downside to social media. Hackers stealing your account, hijacking and cloning your account but you never had an account to clone, so… I'm not sure what's going on here. Unless someone found that photo on the internet and used it to set up a profile. Usually scammers do that. One time I inquired about the cutest puppy and almost sent them a deposit and then someone said they'd stolen that photo off the internet and was using it to scam poor souls who just wanted a furry friend. Tragic." She sighed.

"Well, why would someone use my photo to scam someone?"

"I don't know that they did. There's no activity on the page. Just your profile picture and that you created an account last month. July twentieth." She shrugged. "No one has posted on your wall. Nothing mentioning you selling anything." She sighed. "For two seconds I was excited to see you acting your age. I thought maybe I could convince you to open a dating app too."

"I refuse to do that. I don't care if it's the thing. I don't have time to swipe and hand roses out and all the things. I barely have time for in-person real life."

Laurie sighed. "I can report it. It's probably a bot or something."

"Let me see it again." She took Laurie's phone and looked at the photo of herself. "That's at the community softball games from last month. Who on earth took my photo?" She tried to think back to the games and anyone she might have waved at. She studied her clothing. White shorts and a T-shirt that said Sub-a-Dub-Dub. Eat the Food Truck Grub. Laurie had the shirt made for her birthday this past April.

The photo and profile unsettled her. Her life had been put somewhere public for anyone to see and interact with. And unless Laurie had seen it, she'd have never known she was out there being misrepresented. If anyone friended this "Sadie" they'd be friending a mistaken identity. A fake. "How did you find the fake me?"

"Oh, it showed as a suggested friend in my feed. See." She showed her. "I reported it."

"Can you screenshot it? In case they take it down, I want proof it was there."

Laurie laughed and screenshotted the profile. "Why?"

"I don't know." Something felt…off. Her nerves hummed. Then it hit her.

She remembered waving. And she remembered having her picture taken. She had smiled even wider.

Ben Armstrong had been doing yet another side hustle and photographing the softball games for the Parks and Recreation website. He was techy like that.

Techy enough to set up a fake profile.

As much as she didn't want to rely on Rocco or crawl out from the hole she'd dug with her words and their tiff, she needed him to know this.

She hit his name in her phone and sent a text.

I'm pretty sure I know who's trying to kill me.

# FOURTEEN

Ben Armstrong? Rocco paced in the living room of Laurie Bennett's house. He'd looked at the fake social media profile and Sadie was positive she remembered Ben taking the photos at the softball game last month. She thought it was going to be for the Elk Valley Parks and Recreation section on their website and showcase her food truck.

Why would Ben create a fake profile of Sadie? "He's been doing some work for Jack Norwood. I wonder if he put him up to this? If so, what would be the motive?"

Sadie held her thumbnail between her teeth as she perched on Laurie's couch. Laurie had taken Myles to the play yard at a local fast-food joint. None of them thought his little ears should be privy to the conversation. He'd been through some scary moments already.

When Sadie had texted over twenty minutes ago, his heart had lurched and he thought she might be texting to apologize for the ice earlier. He'd struck a nerve; she was going through so much and the pressure was pushing in on her. It was only a matter of time before she lost her cool. He didn't expect it to be directed at him.

But then she was also feeling things for him. She'd already admitted that and she was fighting them as much as he was fighting his for her.

"I'm going to call Ben in and talk. Just ask him, but at the PD so he knows I'm not joking around with him." He looked around Laurie's house. "In the meantime, you stay put."

"No." She stood. "I want to go with you. Not in the interview room but I want to be there or stand behind the mirror. Hear it for myself."

"That only happens in movies and maybe books. I'm not much of a fiction reader. Point is that isn't going to happen but you can be at the precinct." Probably be safer there anyway. "I can drop you at the food truck later for the dinner shift. I have a video call at noon, though."

She glanced up, her mouth hanging open. "After I unloaded on you earlier?"

He sighed. "It's called grace, Sadie. I know you didn't mean to get up in my grill like that. It's not who you are."

Her eyes filled with moisture. "I appreciate it. I am sorry. I just... I don't know. Thanks."

Rocco had Jamie call Ben in and they drove to the PD in silence. Sadie waited in the reception area with a cup of pretty bad coffee and Rocco met Jamie outside the interview room. Ben had been down the street at the fire department, volunteering. He was already inside the interview room, bobbing his leg and looking around.

Jamie and Rocco watched from the one-way window, making him wait and sweat a little. "I told him we had a few questions we wanted to ask about Sadie Owens and he was quick to come in but he looks anything but calm to me," Jamie said. "What do you think?"

"That he's nervous. Antsy. But that could be for any reason." Rocco sighed. "You taking lead?"

"Nah, you do it. You know you'd make a great detective and the testing comes up in winter. You should consider it." Jamie grinned. "Let's go talk to this guy."

He wasn't going to consider more responsibility until he helped catch the RMK as well as the person setting fires and killing people. He had to put all his energy into that.

Rocco opened the door and Ben glanced up, visibly relaxing to see him. "Hey, man. Is Sadie okay?"

"She's hanging in." He sat in one of the two chairs across from Ben. Jamie took the other seat. He'd saved the profile picture of Sadie on his phone and showed it to Ben. "Do you remember taking this photo at the softball game last month?"

Ben nodded. "Yeah. I took a bunch of photos for the Parks and Rec section of the Elk Valley website. Side gig."

"After you took these, what did you do with them?" Rocco asked.

Cocking his head, he frowned. "I edited them then uploaded and sent them to the Parks and Rec director."

"Tina Chambers." Lee's sister.

"That's right. She paid me three hundred dollars."

"Did you do anything else with them?" Rocco asked.

"No. Why would I? What's going on?" Ben asked.

Rocco exchanged glances with Jamie and Jamie nodded. Rocco showed Ben the profile attributed to Sadie along with the photo. "Because this is Sadie's profile pic and Sadie didn't create this. She doesn't have any personal social media accounts. Just a little website about the food truck and the menu. One photo of her truck and some of the food she serves. Did you create the profile—and before you answer, we have tech analysts who can find out. So tell the truth now."

Ben scowled and pushed back his chair, the legs scraping against the tile floor. "Why would I do that? It makes no sense. Have anyone you want check. I didn't create a fake profile of Sadie Owens. I don't know anyone who would. I did a job. That's all. Rocco, you know me."

"I know you've been pretty tight with Jack Norwood lately."

"Jack throws me business and I need all the money I can get. My sister is sick. She doesn't have insurance. I'm trying to help her out. She lives in Jackson Hole. You can call her if you want. I send her money every week. That's the truth."

Rocco didn't know Ben's sister well. "I'm sorry to hear that. We're not accusing you. We're just trying to do our jobs. You're around a lot. You have access to turpentine. You're a volunteer for the fire department. You see how these little dots connect, don't you?"

"Yeah. But they don't connect to Sadie Owens or anyone else. I volunteer because it's the right thing to do. I told you why I had turpentine. I'm not some arsonist and I'm sure no murderer." He stood. "And I really can't afford an attorney, but I guess I'll get one because I'm not answering any more questions, Rocco. I'm assuming I'm free to go if you're not charging me."

"You're free to go for now," Jamie said. "One last question. Did the Parks and Rec team upload that photo of Sadie to their website?"

"Yes. She's a staple in Elk Valley. You can access the website and see for yourself. Anyone could have taken that photo from their site and used it. Your suspect pool just grew." He walked out of the interview room and Rocco balled his fist.

"He's right. Anyone could have downloaded her photo and used it for the social media profile."

"I'll have Isla see if she can find out who created it." Jamie stood. "For now, we keep a close eye on Ben."

Rocco met up with Sadie in the reception area and shook his head. "That photo of you is on the Elk Valley website. Anyone could have taken it. It might be Ben but I don't know for sure. If it is, he's a pretty good liar."

"I wish I knew why someone made a profile page with

my name and photo. Maybe it was a random scammer. I saw Isla. She said Jamie texted her to find out who created it—or at least the IP address. She said she'd get to the bottom of it. I don't even want to know what she's going to do."

"Isla is very talented but she'd never cross a legal line," he said. "The fake profile might be nothing or it could be something. I'm going to have her see if fake profiles have been created on our other victims. Maybe this is a link." He hoped they would get a break. "You going to hang out here?"

"No. I'm going to walk down the block on a very public sidewalk with shoppers and go to my food truck."

"I'll check in later." He held her gaze a moment, wondering if she meant those words she'd said earlier about him minding his own business and leaving her out of it. He went into the conference room. Chase was already at the head of the table with his laptop open, brooding. His dark eyes concentrating on the screen.

"Hey," Rocco said. "Thought I'd just come in for the MCK-9 briefing since I was already here. No point phoning in. That cool?"

Chase nodded. "Yeah, You get a lead on the arson case?"

"Maybe." He filled him in and then Isla entered with rookie Ashley Hanson and Hannah Scott, the state trooper from Utah. Hannah and Meadow had driven in, for a personal meeting later with Chase about protecting Trevor who was living in Salt Lake City. They greeted him and took seats across from Chase.

"Rest of the team will be on Zoom," Chase said. "I have it running through the projector so we can all see them." One by one team members popped on and began making small talk, catching up and joking around. Meadow asked Rocco about the arson case and he briefed them.

Chase called the meeting to order. "We've got a major lead on Cowgirl."

"Awesome," Meadow said. "Is she safe? Well?"

Chase raked a hand through his hair. "A labradoodle with a dark splotch on her ear has been spotted again in Salt Lake City with the tall blond guy wearing sunglasses. So it's good news and bad news."

"Trevor Gage lives in Salt Lake," Rocco said. "And the killer left that note saying he was saving the best for last." They inferred that meant Trevor since he was the one who had pranked Naomi Carr-Cavanaugh by inviting her to the dance that night under false pretenses.

Chase nodded. "It means this might be his final target, so we can breathe easier knowing that. But it also means Trevor's life is in jeopardy and we aren't sure who we're looking for. Evan Carr. Ryan York. Someone else. Thing is if he is gunning for him then he's probably hidden away a stack of cash and will go underground. We can't let that happen. We can't let him disappear."

The team agreed.

"We're going to Salt Lake City and catch him. As of now, Hannah, you're already based there, so that's a given. Isla, you, Rocco and I can drive in so we'll each have our vehicles. I know you have a major case going on here, Rocco. You've got some time. If you need an extra hand, I'm in. But I need you there when it's time."

Rocco didn't want to leave Sadie to go to Salt Lake if the case wasn't wrapped up. He would convince her to go to the cabin and he'd have Jamie Watershed look out for her, but that wasn't the same as Rocco's protection. He was invested. In the case *and* Sadie and Myles.

And that terrified him.

"I appreciate that, Chase. Thanks." He didn't want to debate about not going in front of the team. He'd discuss it later if it came to that.

Once Chase dismissed the team, Rocco talked with Isla and Liana Lightfoot—the dog trainer.

"Hey!" Hannah called as Rocco strode down the hall to the lobby. "I wanted to talk to you a minute. In private."

"Sure."

They fell into step together. "I've been trying to persuade Trevor to go into a safe house but so far he's resisted. He's too out in the open like you said, and this killer is slippery."

"I agree. He's eluded us far too long."

"I have my doubts about what is true or not about that dance ten years ago. Did Trevor really ask Naomi to the dance as a cruel joke?" Her eyes held skepticism.

"I hope not." But so many mean pranks had been pulled and it was obvious not all those guys had grown up or out of them. Lee Chambers and his crew came to mind. "In all Trevor's interviews over the past several months he's held the claim that he actually liked Naomi and it wasn't a joke, but his friends twisted it out of hand. But sometimes people lie and they're good at it." None of the team knew if Trevor was being honest or not.

"Let's pray we find the killer before he finds Trevor— especially if he won't go into a safe house," Hannah said. "And I'll pray you solve this arson/homicide before Chase calls you in. I saw your face. You aren't happy about leaving right now. I'll keep my thoughts as to why to myself."

He appreciated that but she was right.

He'd wish Sadie would go into a safe house as well.

Sadie had walked to the food truck, knowing a killer was out there with his sights set on her, but she'd pressed on with her chin up and shoulders back to give an illusion of bravery. No fear.

Inside, she was riddled with terror and anxiety. Once she relieved Blanca of her lunch shift, she stayed busy working on prepping the supper shift and didn't dwell on the nightmare that consumed her life at the moment.

Until Hunter rapped on the side of the truck, startling her.

"What are you doing here?" she asked.

"I wanted to talk to you but you haven't texted or called, so I thought I'd try again in person." His bright eyes and long lashes had once stunned her heart but not anymore. He'd shown his true colors in too many ways to count. "I'm leaving for Jackson Hole in two days. I wanted to see my kid."

Was he joking? "When will you be coming back to Elk Valley?"

"I don't know. I'm taking a job helping on a ranch there." He shrugged.

"So you want to spend one hour with Myles and then leave for months. You can't pop in and out of his life, Hunter. And I'm not convinced you had nothing to do with these fires. It would make your life pretty easy if we weren't around. No child support hanging over your head."

His eyes narrowed. "There it is. You don't want me to see my son because I haven't paid you for the time."

Sadie seethed but inhaled deeply and let out a slow, measured breath. "You don't see your son because his diabetes was too hard for you to deal with. It's not about paying for his time. It's about you don't parent, period. You don't call him. You don't make trips to visit. You don't even call and ask *me* about him. Why do you want to see him now?"

"You think I'm trying to kill you?" His tone was venomous and his eyes slits. "Have you lost your mind? Are you delusional?"

"Are you?" He thought he could show up and see Myles, which would open up a conversation she had no clue to navigate with a three-year-old. Hunter hadn't seen him since he was six months old and he'd been to town a handful of times to see his parents. This wasn't fair to Myles.

"You know if you do sell your business to Jack, it would take care of your financial problems."

How would he even know about that? He'd been working for Jack. Jack must have spilled the tea in order to get Hunter to encourage her to sell to that snake. He didn't want to see Myles. He wanted to create an environment where he could appear changed and coax her to sell because it benefited Hunter. If Sadie was financially set, she wouldn't be tempted to take Hunter to court. He was equally a snake.

"I see now. You may have deceived me before, but not again. You cannot see Myles. You don't truly want to anyway. That's why you're here now. You know I'll never let you into his life to hurt him the way you hurt me. You need to leave right now. I'm not selling anything to anyone. I don't want your money. You wrote us off and we've been fine without you." She pulled the window closed and collapsed on the bench, tears stinging the backs of her eyes.

She snatched her phone. Her decision had been made. She would not sell her business or recipes. Jack had stooped super low by enlisting Hunter to use their son to manipulate her. She texted him in all caps.

I WILL NEVER SELL MY BUSINESS. IF YOU APPROACH ME AGAIN I WILL TAKE OUT A RESTRAINING ORDER FOR HARASSMENT OR RETAIN A LAWYER TO SEEK LEGAL ACTION. I KNOW PEOPLE TOO, MR. NORWOOD.

Then she blocked his number and leaned her head against

the wall. Then it dawned on her what she'd done. What if Jack was the killer, she'd all but threw down the gauntlet to finish the job. The dam burst as tears erupted, her only prayers because words would not do. She might have made a grave mistake.

When they finally dried up, a knock on the doors of her truck sounded. "Sadie, it's Rocco."

Sadie opened the door and his smile faded when he saw her face. "Do I look that bad?" she asked.

He stepped inside the truck, Cocoa following, and held her hands. "What happened?"

She unloaded on him. "I blocked him after I texted, so who knows what he's thinking. I shouldn't have been so impulsive. I should have thought it through. If he shows up——"

"I'll arrest him for harassment." He hugged her and she pushed away. She could not let herself depend on him, rely on him...love him. "I'm sorry," he said, his face pained.

"I think we need to stick to friendship at best. I appreciate all you've done and are doing, but it's just too hard."

His Adam's apple bobbed and he nodded. "I understand."

Did he? She didn't even fully understand why she was pushing him away. No, she did.

Fear.

And he'd never asked to try and make a go of things. He'd only reiterated why he couldn't, even if he was feeling things for her. Best to keep a distance, including an innocent hug.

"I'm sorry."

"Don't be. I still think you should consider a safe house and to continue staying at my place until this is solved. Isla is working on finding who set up the fake account. Shouldn't be long but she's had a few other things to attend to. We'll see if it connects to these murders."

She nodded. She knew staying with Rocco was the safest

place for her and Myles. But she needed space. "I'm going to stay at Laurie's. We're literally down the street from the police department. I need… I need a night. Okay?"

He nodded. "If you don't need any help here, I'm going to work the case with Jamie even if it is my day off. Call if you need me. I'm sure you won't, though." He hopped out of the truck and Cocoa followed.

Life was a raging storm right now.

She'd hurt him unintentionally but there was nothing she could do about it now. Instead of dwelling on it, she worked through the dinner crowd. By the time she was finished it was almost seven thirty. The sun hadn't dipped behind the horizon yet, so she walked down the few blocks to Laurie's house, needing the breather and exercise. She'd texted Sadie earlier that she was taking Myles to a kids' movie at the rec center and he'd been excited about popcorn. Sadie had reminded her to make sure Myles didn't feed Dolly any. She used the key to Laurie's house and entered, inhaling vanilla and caramel. Laurie loved the scented candles.

Sadie couldn't remember the last time she'd had alone time. Having already eaten, she changed into a pair of athletic pants and a fresh T-shirt then plopped on the couch and clicked through the streaming services, finding nothing of interest. The last thing she wanted to watch was crime shows or documentaries. Her life felt like one. Except she was pretty sure she didn't light up a room when she entered.

As she curled up on the couch, the reality of how alone she truly was hit her. And the one man who wanted to be a part of her life, she was pushing away. How did that make any sense? Her eyes grew heavy and she let herself drift.

Sadie jolted from the couch. The living room was dark. She checked her cell phone clock and it was almost nine thirty. Laurie had texted she was taking Myles for a fruit pop and to her parents' to catch lightning bugs, and had told her to enjoy the few hours alone. Laurie was the best.

No texts from Rocco.

But something had woken her from sleep. A noise. That was when she heard it again, louder.

Sirens.

Fire truck sirens. She stepped out onto the porch and could smell the smoke from here. Something was on fire down the street. Police cars raced by and neighbors poked their heads from homes like she was doing.

Rocco's truck came up the drive, his face tight and his lips grim.

"What is it?" she asked, coming down the concrete steps.

"Sadie," he said as he exited the truck. "I don't even know how to say this. It's your food truck. It's been torched."

# FIFTEEN

Sadie bolted from Rocco's vehicle. Lights cut through the darkness and a crowd had already gathered, filling the streets with gasps and whispers. The firefighters had put out the flames. Her precious legacy had gone up in smoke and was nothing more than a charred hull. Her dad had handcrafted the sign with the flowers that had hung on the side of the truck.

Now it was all gone.

Everything was gone. Destroyed. She sank to her knees, her heart stuttering and her mind buzzing. Tears blurred her vision and she sobbed in front of the whole community. She didn't even care. Now what was she going to do? No home. No place of business. No income.

A killer wanted her dead.

She'd shoved away the only man who had ever cared about her further than skin-deep.

Dad was gone.

And her son was sick.

Was this a joke? Was God cruel? He could have prevented this but He'd allowed it to happen and whoever did it had gotten away with it too.

A hand rested on her shoulder then Rocco squatted beside her. "I'm so sorry, Sadie. I wish we'd caught this guy already but... I failed you."

She glanced up into his dark eyes. "You're the only person who hasn't failed me."

Rocco ran the pad of his thumb over her cheekbone, swiping a few tears. She was past the breaking point. She'd been loaded with more burdens than anyone should have to be. The weight was crushing.

Ben Armstrong approached with the fire chief. "Can't say for certain about the origin," the chief said. "But we'll find out."

Jamie Watershed approached with a few questions. His last one: "And you can't think of anyone who might want to burn this thing down other than Jack Norwood?"

Sadie told him about Hunter coming by and the heated discussion and then her texting Jack she wasn't ever going to sell her business or recipes and blocking his number.

"Do you keep the recipes in the food truck?" Jamie asked.

"No. They're up here." She pointed to her temple.

"Jack could have been furious once you gave him a final no and then blocked him to boot," Rocco said. "We need to find out where he was tonight. Although someone like him would hire out the dirty work. He'd hate to get his hands stained."

"I'll get on that now." Jamie patted Sadie's shoulder. "I'm real sorry about your food truck."

Neighbors, patrons and many community members began to find her to offer condolences and help, and some came to be nosy, asking questions that were none of their business. Sadie's chest tightened and nerves filled her belly. Invisible walls closed in on her and she pushed through the throng of people to get a break, be alone for five seconds and to gather her thoughts.

"Sadie!" Rocco called.

"Manelli," someone hollered and Rocco turned around.

Sadie pushed through the trees to a bench not far from the street littered with people. They mostly meant well, but Sadie had peopled enough. Laying her head in her hands, she bent forward to take deep cleansing breaths in hopes of warding off a panic attack.

"How much more will You rip from me, Lord?" How much more could she stand? How would she make a living? How long would it take for insurance money to kick in so she could rebuild or move? She didn't want another food truck. She wanted the one her father had left her.

A chill raised hairs on her neck.

She wasn't alone.

She spun around to see Ben Armstrong standing two feet away. "You scared me to death, Ben."

"Did I?" He shrugged. "I'm sorry. I saw you wander off and thought it might not be safe. It's too dark to see you out here. You never know who's lurking or who's been trying to kill you."

She swallowed hard. Something didn't feel right. It was almost like the atmosphere had changed. It was cold. Freezing cold and she shivered. "You're right. I should... I should be getting back."

"Yeah, sure. But—"

Suddenly Ben collapsed to the ground as if he'd had a heart attack. Standing behind him was a man wearing a ski mask, a gun in one hand, now dripping with blood from having bludgeoned Ben. He motioned for her to start walking. "You try anything and I'll not only kill you but I'll kill your kid."

His voice sounded familiar but strange. He darted a glance toward the crowd. "Head for the woods. Now."

Sadie wanted to cry out, to run, but he had a gun and she

had a small boy who needed his mother to be smart and stay alive. "Officer Manelli—"

"Is tied up at the moment with everyone else. No one is looking for you." He motioned with his gun for her to start walking. "You lied to me, Sadie. Led me on. No one leads me on and rejects me."

Sadie opened her mouth to speak and thought better of it. Slowly, she moved in the direction of the woods and the parking lot on the other side of the park. She remembered a self-defense class she'd once taken, where she'd learned that she was never to let her abductor place her in a vehicle and never let them take her to a second location.

But how was she supposed to do that? Her heart rate was racing and her entire body trembled. "Where are we going?"

"Don't play dumb. You know exactly where we're going. It was your idea after all."

Rocco's insides were like melted plastic. This sickened him. If he had caught this guy earlier, Sadie wouldn't be out a business, a piece of her father and her livelihood. When she'd dropped to her knees, Rocco had physically felt her emotional pain. He wanted to take it from her, relieve her from the burden and make what was wrong right.

Yes, she'd rejected him but he'd rejected the idea of them together too. Was it worth this kind of agonizing ache in his chest, the hollowness in his gut? He'd given her space, let her take a few feet of much-needed room, but a warning signaled in his gut.

Isla had called him, and was standing before him talking but he hadn't heard a word she said. Sadie had run to the park bench about thirty feet away. He wanted to run with her.

"Rocco, did you hear me?" Isla asked.

"What? No. Sorry." He let his gaze land on her face.

"I have two things. I know how law officials can get behind on paperwork and entering cases into ViCAP, so I've also been combing through news articles about fires with homicides. I found one in Fort Collins. About an hour away. Richard and Judy Sage. A couple died in a fire at their home this past June. Accelerant was turpentine. I talked to one of the criminal investigations detectives and he said it was the only arson-homicide in the town and their first arson altogether."

"What do we know about the couple?" Rocco asked.

"That's the thing. They have zero ties to our victims or even to Elk Valley. No family here or friends or businesses."

But they might connect to their killer.

"They were an upstanding family in the community, heavily involved in their church. Even three decades of fostering children. I'm going to call their only biological daughter and see if she can bring some new light to the situation."

Rocco nodded. "And the other thing."

"I found who set up the social media account. Lee Chambers."

Why would Lee create a fake profile for Sadie? "Anything else?"

"Not yet. And it could take a little while, but I'll dig into all this further."

"Appreciated," Rocco said. "Hopefully I can get Lee to squeal."

"I'll work on gathering evidence to get a search warrant to access the account and see if the fake Sadie had any private conversations with anyone." Rocco nodded, then he glanced up to check on Sadie who'd been sitting on the park bench.

But she was gone.

His stomach lurched and he bolted, leaving Isla calling after him. He sprinted across the street, Cocoa right beside him. Ben Armstrong was lying in a heap, his head bleeding. With all the commotion and under the canvas of night, no one would have seen an altercation under the trees.

He bent and shook him. "Ben. Ben."

Ben came to. "What's going on?"

Rocco radioed paramedics. "Can you tell me what happened?"

"I saw Sadie out here alone and came to tell her she needed to return to the crowd but someone knocked me on the head. I didn't see him. He came from behind."

Paramedics came running to the park.

"It's okay, Ben. I need to find Sadie." Rocco had only taken his eyes off Sadie for a few seconds. He should have never allowed her space.

Cocoa circled and sat behind Ben. He'd detected accelerant.

Maybe the scent would carry and Cocoa could find the trail leading to the killer and Sadie. "Good boy. Now, track, Cocoa."

Cocoa rose to his paws and began sniffing the ground and moving at a clipped pace, Rocco right beside him. He paused at the snow cone stand then caught the scent and moved forward through the dark park. Rocco's flashlight gave him enough light to follow the trail.

Had the killer used this newest fire to draw her out, keep them busy and open up an opportunity to abduct her? How would he know she would go into the park?

He must have stuck around, blending into the crowd— clearly not an outsider. An outsider would have been noticed. Rocco had seen Ben Armstrong, Lee Chambers and Jack Norwood in the crowd. He hadn't had time to talk to Jack yet but he would. Sadie had blown him off and blocked him. He would be furious.

Lee had set up that stupid account without Sadie knowing.

Cocoa led Rocco to the small wooded parking lot that was now empty. He trotted to the edge of the lot to the last parking space and circled then sat. This must be where he'd been parked.

He was gone.

And he had Sadie.

Rocco patted Cocoa's head and they jogged back through the park. He called Jamie and told him what had happened and the news Isla had given him a few minutes ago. "Wake up a judge. We now have all the evidence we need for a search warrant into that account and we need to question Lee Chambers right now."

"I agree. I'll call him."

"He's here. I saw him in the crowd earlier."

"He's not here now. Most everyone is gone now that the drama has died down. In fact, all our suspects are gone."

Which meant any one of them could have her.

Thirty minutes later, Lee Chambers sat inside the interview room at Elk Valley PD. Rocco sat across from him and Jamie beside Rocco. Lee's jaw was tight and his nostrils flaring but his balled hand rubbed up and down his thigh.

He was nervous.

Rocco slid the printed copy of the fake profile across the table, his own nerves about to cause him to come unglued. Sadie was missing. Laurie hadn't seen her or talked to her. Rocco had recommended Laurie stay with Myles at her parents' house to be safe. He couldn't be sure the killer wouldn't come for Myles.

He'd called Sadie's phone multiple times but it had been turned off. Going straight to voice mail.

"What is this?" Lee asked, grit and fury in his voice.

"You know what it is, Lee. We've traced this fake profile of Sadie directly to your laptop. You can tell us why you did it, if you messaged anyone—or if anyone messaged you, or we can secure a warrant for your laptop and phone and we'll find what we're looking for the hard way."

Lee sat back. "Then get a warrant."

Rocco bit back his own fury and swallowed it down. "Lee, Sadie has never wronged you. Not once. And she's missing. Someone has had it out for her and is wrecking her life and if this fake profile has anything to do with it, now is the time to cough it up, because securing a warrant takes more time than we have—than Sadie has. Do you want a little boy to go into foster care? That's what will happen if you don't get it together and help us."

Although Rocco knew if something terrible happened to Sadie—God forbid—he'd want Myles. His diabetes didn't scare him. He loved the boy.

And…he loved Sadie. Maybe he had for a very long time. After all he did eat at her truck every day not only because the food was good but because it was a chance to see her. Talk with her. Get to know her. She was genuinely kind and compassionate. Strong and intelligent. And he was over the moon at her snark and sass.

He'd been a total idiot.

He was putting cold cases above something red-hot right in front of him now. Why couldn't he do both? Find the balance his father didn't? Instead of being afraid of becoming his father—which he had in his obsession with the RMK—he could focus on being present personally and professionally.

"Sadie's cool." Lee's hardened features softened. "It was a joke. Not on her."

Jokes and pranks had a history of causing homicides in this town. Cruelty had wrecked families and this community. "Haven't you learned what happens to people who are the victims of cruel jokes, Lee? You were friends with Seth, Aaron and Brad. You knew the most recent victims of the RMK as well. Peter, Henry and Luke. The killer is still out there and we're hunting him, but word on the street is that the RMK is targeting those who humiliated Naomi at the dance ten years ago. Words and actions matter, Lee. People get hurt and that leads to bitterness, which leads to revenge."

Lee sighed and raked a hand through his hair. "You're right, Manelli. I was angry. I get angry sometimes."

"You're quoting a line from the Hulk? Really?"

"Well, it's true. I want a deal. I'll tell the truth but I don't want to be charged with anything."

Rocco snorted. "Unbelievable. You want to do rotten things with no consequences? There are consequences to every action, Lee. You don't get to escape them. Either tell us right now what happened, and your involvement, or Sadie is going to die. Do you want that over your head? That your behavior caused a murder. What did you do?"

Lee hung his head, remaining quiet as the seconds ticked by. Each one another second Sadie might be suffering…and dying. Finally he looked up and Rocco saw the remorse in his eyes.

About time.

"We never meant for Sadie to get hurt. We just wanted to teach him a lesson."

"Who? Who did you want to teach a lesson?"

# SIXTEEN

Sadie closed her eyes and prayed God would save her. He hadn't saved her home or her business but she had a little boy who needed her. Her bound hands trembled behind her back as she was forced out of the truck by the masked man.

He hadn't answered any of her questions or spoken a peep since forcing her inside the black Ford truck with damage on the bumper and sides. The same truck that had tried to run them off roads. She hadn't recognized it and she wasn't sure she knew who had kidnapped her but his voice earlier had been familiar, only harsher and grittier. She'd been trying to place it since he'd held her at gunpoint.

"Please let me go. I have a son. Surely you know this. I'm all he has in this whole world and he's sick. I know how to take care of him. Please, I'm begging you," she pleaded. Maybe he wasn't a monster but a man who had some small sliver of compassion or mercy.

"You say you love him, but you don't. You'll abandon him. In the end, he won't be able to trust anyone but himself. People lie. People leave," he said with a biting tone.

That voice. Her mind shuffled through memories trying to capture the man behind it.

Mountains loomed like frightening giants as he drove

them out of Elk Valley and toward Medicine Bow National Forest. "Where are we going?"

"You know exactly where we're going."

No. She didn't, but she considered it wise not to protest. "Why did you set my house and my food truck on fire? Why did you kill Coach Towers and Herman Willows?"

The curves sharpened and he handled them as if he'd made them often. "Coach Towers was a bully in teacher's clothing. He could have made me pitcher. I was good enough, but he didn't. Instead he gave the position to someone else. And Herman... Herman knew I had better business sense than any other employee but did he make me assistant manager when I asked? No. My whole life has been nothing but people rejecting me and leaving me standing around like a fool. They got what they deserved."

What had Sadie done? "Take off your mask."

He turned down a road that cut into the Rocky Mountains and narrowed as it climbed upward until he turned left down a hidden road. Up ahead she saw a small rectangular cabin with a wraparound porch. He parked the truck. "We can't do what we originally planned since it's nighttime. But we can do the other thing."

Sadie swallowed. "What other thing?" she whispered.

He turned on the interior lights and she squinted. He slowly removed his ski mask and she gasped.

So unexpected.

Confusion overwhelmed her and she shook her head as Bobby Linton sat in the driver's seat. "You know what other thing."

"I'm afraid I don't, Bobby. I don't have a single clue what is happening or why you feel I've rejected you the way others have."

Bobby banged his fist on the steering wheel, the horn

honking. "Stop lying to me! Stop acting like you don't know me. Like you didn't lead me on then ghost me!" he bellowed.

She shrank back and wished for hands to defend herself. A vein in his forehead bulged and his face was redder than a hot poker. He picked up the gun and tears streaked down her cheeks. "Bobby, I'm not sure what has happened but we can talk it out. Make it right."

"Oh, I'm making it right. Now. You and me are going in that cabin and you're cooking for me just like you promised. A nice meal at my cabin, hiking through the Medicine Bow National Forest to relax in nature. I let the first time you stood me up go. But not this time. Not after all your begging forgiveness. I believed your son was sick. Still, I was humiliated as I left the restaurant by Lee and his minions who laughed and jested about me being stood up. I tried to give you another chance. I followed your rules to act like we never had hours of conversations and a connection. You'll do this and then I'll decide what to do with you."

Sadie's mind whirled. What was Bobby talking about?

"Out of the truck. Now." He hauled her across the cab and out of his driver's-side door. With a gun pressed to her back, he forced her up the porch steps, then he unlocked the door and shoved her inside.

It hit her then.

The fake social media profile someone had created. They'd used it to have conversations with Bobby and make dates that she broke. Why? Why would someone use her to hurt Bobby? To create this elaborate and cruel joke on him.

The night light under the microwave illuminated the open-concept cabin. Old, worn furniture. A rustic kitchen and paintings of nature and wildlife made the place homey—if she wasn't a prisoner here. Should she tell him he'd been catfished? Would it cause him to apologize or would he feel the greater fool and kill her anyway? He clearly had a volatile temper. If she provoked him in any way, he'd be even more dangerous and unpredictable.

"Remind me again of what I'm cooking. And do you have the ingredients?" Better to play along and look for an opportunity to escape.

Because she would find one. She wasn't staying here with this man any longer than she absolutely had to.

"Bobby Linton?" Rocco asked Lee. "What did Bobby ever do to you that you would play a horrible prank on him and why are you using Sadie?" It was all Rocco could do to keep from coming across the table and throttling this guy.

"So we were at a game in early July and Bobby was there—not playing. He hasn't played since Coach chose me to pitch over him. Threw such a baby tantrum, carrying on about playing favorites and treating him like trash, passing him over and whatever. But he did come to the games and to our community league ones. He was sitting next to my girl, Andrea, and talking with her. I saw the way he looked at her."

Rocco remembered Sadie mentioning this. She'd said Bobby wasn't staring at Andrea and that Lee was being a real bully. She'd given Bobby free nachos and kindness to lick his wounds. The scene had been humiliating. "Sadie said he wasn't looking at her in any way but being nice."

"I don't care what Sadie said. He was talking to my woman and eyeing her, and it hadn't been the first time. Not to mention the guy is a total wack job. He freaks everyone out, including Andrea and her friends."

Rocco held his temper in check. "That doesn't give you the right to treat him like a piece of garbage. What exactly did you do, Lee? And give me the short version. Sadie's life is at stake because of you."

Lee huffed. "Look, I downloaded a photo of Sadie and created a personal profile then I messaged Bobby and asked if he was okay and if he liked the nachos. I let Bobby believe Sadie was into him. They had several conversations over messenger and—"

"Pull it up on your phone right this second," Rocco demanded and Lee obeyed and slid his phone across the table. Rocco scrolled through two weeks of messages, each one becoming more personal. Small talk to Bobby revealing private things about his life. How he never knew his father—his own mom didn't know who had fathered him, to his mom giving him up at four years old. He'd cycled in and out of the foster care system until he landed with the Sage family.

The Sage family.

That was the couple in Fort Collins who had died in a fire in June. They'd fostered children. Had one daughter of their own.

Rocco continued reading Bobby's messages. Bobby had thought he was going to have a loving home but the daughter didn't like him and they'd sent him back into the foster care system after he'd been in their home almost two years. From this, Bobby felt abandoned and he ended up having some very bad experiences in the new foster homes. Always being cycled from place to place until he finished out in a boys' home and they kicked him out at eighteen.

He'd been on his own since then.

Lee, pretending to be Sadie, had been sympathetic in her replies, stating he didn't deserve that and she wanted to hug him and make him feel better. Lee's responses sickened Rocco as it gave Bobby, who clearly had rejection and abandonment issues, hope that Sadie cared for him romantically.

"How did he not approach Sadie in all these weeks?" Rocco muttered as he and Jamie scrolled through the messages. He paused to text Isla to look into Bobby Linton's foster years and in connection to the Sage family. She was already going to call the daughter. Maybe she had already.

"Sadie told him that her son had been rejected by his father too and she understood but she didn't want anyone to know they were talking because she wanted things to go well before Myles found out. He bought it. I had no idea he'd torch her house and food truck and kidnap her," Lee said.

"Anyone with half a brain can tell he's unstable from these messages. The animosity and hate he feels toward those who he believes rejected him or passed him over or humiliated him. You were creating the perfect storm!"

Lee Chambers was an idiot who deserved prison time for his part in this whole scam.

Rocco's phone rang. Isla. He stepped out into the hall. "What do you have? Tell me something."

"I talked to Patty Wingate—the Sages' daughter. According to her, Bobby was violent when he was angry. Her parents tried. He was ten years old and causing trouble. They put him in counseling and prayed for him daily but they're sure he hurt a neighbor's cat, and when he was twelve, he pushed Patty down a flight of stairs and she broke her arm. They'd been through quite an ordeal in the two years they'd committed to him but her safety was priority. She said it was the hardest thing her parents ever did, but she was relieved because whenever he was angry, he was devious and physically violent."

He hoped and prayed Sadie wouldn't anger him. But when one was this unstable no one could determine what crossed the line. "Anything else?"

"Yeah. She said the first week of June they ran into him while hiking in the Medicine Bow National Forest. Actually, she said he followed them and it was scary because, at first, they didn't realize who he was. He approached them around ten that morning and then they saw him again around noon. Once her mother figured it out they spoke to him. Asked how he was, but she said they were afraid."

"Did he accost them?"

"No. Just said he hiked out there often. Had a cabin nearby. After, he left but Patty says she felt like he was stalking them from the woods. Felt his eyes on them. Two weeks later, her parents died in a fire at their home. She always suspected Bobby and even gave the police his name. They talked to him. His alibi was that he was at the cabin alone. No other evidence supported he did it, so they couldn't charge him."

Unbelievable.

Coach had passed him over.

The Sages had rejected him—in his unstable mind.

Sadie—from the messages—had stood him up for dinner at a restaurant, apologized and promised to cook him dinner at his cabin.

"Isla, can you get me that cabin's address?"

"Give me...just...got it." She relayed the address and he typed it into his phone.

"Thanks." He ended the call and entered the interview room, looking at Lee. "You're going nowhere until I know Sadie is safe."

Jamie followed him into the hall and Rocco relayed Isla's words. "Let me send backup with you."

"No. He sees cops and he could kill her."

"Then at least let me go with you. Just the two of us. Be smart about this."

He nodded. Jamie had an officer escort Lee to a cell for holding while he and Rocco and Cocoa jumped in Rocco's truck and headed for Bobby's cabin.

Hopefully, he wouldn't be too late.

# SEVENTEEN

Sadie had apparently promised Bobby pasta carbonara and a salad. He'd purchased the groceries and she was boiling water and cooking the pancetta and garlic, her hands trembling. Bobby leaned against the wall, the gun pointed at her now that she was unbound.

"I'm sorry about burning down your truck, Sadie. I was so mad and I knew you'd come out. I knew everyone would, and I was hoping for the chance to get you. I'm still mad. Why would you say those things to me and let me vent to you about my life only to treat me like I don't exist?" He was becoming angry again and it reflected in the volume of his voice and biting tone.

She had no idea what had been said to him on her behalf or what the point had been. What she did know was that Myles was safe and Rocco was searching for her and he would find her. She had no doubt.

"Smells good," he said softly, switching from agitated to kind.

"What happens now? I mean after dinner." What was he going to do? Maybe she could convince him that she was sorry and would never tell. Then she could make an escape and find Rocco. Because she knew Bobby had murdered people and set fires. He'd admitted it all firsthand.

"I understand why you did it. To get my attention. It worked, Bobby." She needed to play this cool. Calculate a plan. "Have you ever been scared of anything?" she asked.

"Of course I have. You know this."

Except she didn't. "Then you know why I didn't show. Cold feet and fear of rejection. You know what my ex did to me."

Bobby cocked his head, his bright blue eyes studying her to discern if she was full of it or being honest. "No, I don't really. You never shared too much with me."

Because whoever had been sharing didn't know the deep parts of her life and couldn't reveal too much. Not without being questioned or caught.

"Well, Hunter wasn't the nicest guy. I mean, he never hurt me. Never hit me. But he cheated then made me think I was dreaming it up, and I believed him because it was easier than knowing I wasn't enough for him. Knowing that his son wasn't enough either. He walked out on us when we found out Myles had diabetes. I understand rejection and abandonment and betrayal—but I didn't betray you. I just… I was afraid to take that next step. I was afraid you might walk out too. Maybe not at first but eventually."

Which was why she had pushed Rocco away.

"I would never do that. I've been there and you should have known you could count on me. I'd never betray you, Sadie. Or Myles. He's a cute kid."

So cute he'd nearly killed him three times.

"Let's just…let's start over. Can we?" he asked.

She swallowed the mountain of terror in her throat and nodded, tears filming her eyes and blurring him. "Yeah," she managed. She turned the burner on low to not burn the garlic and pancetta. The pot of water began to bubble but hadn't come to a rolling boil yet.

He approached her and kneaded her neck with his free hand. It chilled her skin and caused a shiver.

"What? Why are you flinching at my touch?" His hand tightened on her shoulder.

"I'm just nervous. You're holding a gun on me, Bobby. Could you put it away?"

He sighed and nodded. "That's fair." He shoved it in his waistband and placed both hands on her shoulders, rubbing lovingly, but in her mind it might as well be brown recluse spiders skittering along her skin. She bit down on her bottom lip to keep from flinching or wincing. She had no excuse now.

He leaned in, his warm breath on her neck. "Smells delicious." He pressed his nose into her hair. "You smell good too."

She glanced at the stockpot of water rolling to a boil.

Now or never.

He brushed her hair aside and kissed her neck. She grabbed the handles of the pot and swung around, throwing it into his face. Some of the scalding water splashed onto her arms and she yelped as he let out a wail, his face and neck blistering, his chest soaked.

Sadie grabbed his gun from his waistband and raced for the front door, throwing it open and bolting down the porch. From behind, she heard his bellowing and cursing her and then the sounds of his footfalls on the porch. He was chasing her, but he wouldn't be able to see her well—or at all. She had a fighting chance.

She ran and smacked into a tree in the middle of the road.

Not a tree.

A person.

She held the gun out.

"Whoa! Whoa! Put that down. It's me, Sadie. It's me."

Rocco.

She'd never been so relieved. "It's Bobby. He's after me."

"I got him." Detective Watershed bolted from the shadows and sprinted toward the cabin.

Rocco took the gun from her, shoved it in his waistband and cupped her face. "Did he hurt you?"

She shook her head. "I threw boiling water at him." She fell into Rocco, inhaling his soapy scent and his strength. She was safe. "I was so scared. He mistook that fake profile for the real me. Thought I had been the one behind a romantic online relationship." She clung to him and melted into his embrace and his touch, relishing his lips against her forehead. No flinching or wincing.

Only security, strength and solace.

"I know. Lee Chambers was behind it." Rocco kissed her brow. "I'm going to help Jamie. You stay behind that tree. I'll come get you."

She nodded and ducked behind a tree as Rocco darted but then paused. "Sadie."

"Yeah?"

"We have some talking to do because I love you."

Her heart skittered and her cheeks flushed but then he was gone in the night and she was left with her reply on her tongue.

She loved him too.

Not only loved him but completely trusted him.

And they did have a lot to talk about.


Rocco watched Sadie sip a cup of coffee as daybreak dawned. Last night, Jamie had secured Bobby Linton and gotten him medical attention. He had second-degree burns which were being treated, and his sight would be salvageable. Once he was released, he'd be charged with the arsons and homicides of four people and the attempted murder of Sadie, Myles and Rocco as well as kidnapping.

Bobby was going away a long, long time.

Case closed.

As it turned out, Jack wasn't behind any of it and Ben and Hunter had been telling the truth. Rusty Remington was shady and a criminal, but he'd actually been speaking truth about his time in Elk Valley.

In just a few days, Rocco would be leaving for Salt Lake City to catch the Rocky Mountain Killer who was there targeting Trevor Gage—saving the best for last. But they'd find him. They were on to him. Ryan York? Evan Carr? Or someone else with blond hair and a labradoodle who had a dark splotch on her ear. And the culprit who had it out for Isla was still hiding in the shadows. The threats against her had escalated to arson—attempted murder since she'd been in the house—and they had no leads.

Rocco didn't want to leave, but this case needed to be solved. He wasn't going to let it consume him like it had for so long. He wanted a healthy balance of being in law enforcement and having a life—a family of his own.

And he wanted it with Sadie.

After bringing her back to his ranch last night, they'd been exhausted. It had been well after midnight, so he hadn't approached the subject of how much he loved her.

But now was a different story.

"Hey," he said quietly.

She startled then smiled. He could get used to this face every morning. "Hey," she said.

"Did you sleep at all?"

"I actually did. First time in a while, and Myles too. I've been praying this wouldn't negatively affect him. Guess God is answering that prayer. I got an email from the insurance company and it's going to be enough to buy a new home and purchase a new food truck and pay off medical bills. Guess God had a plan—could have done without the drama but I'm grateful."

"I've found God works everything—including attempted murders and arson—out for the good of those who love Him. Making good out of bad. But I hear ya." She could buy a new truck but it wouldn't be the same truck.

"I'm glad I didn't sell. And I also have some catering requests too."

He approached her. "We make a good team—catering. Cooking. I'd like to see us be a good team in life. I meant it when I said it, Sadie. I love you. And I love Myles. I even love Dolly."

She grinned. "It's a lot taking on both of us."

"No, it's not. But I need to know... I need to know—"

"I love you... *Rocco*."

Those words were like the sun shining after a bitterly cold day. A smile slid across his face and he pulled her into his arms. "You didn't sound under duress."

"I wasn't. I'm not." She mimicked his grin. "I was afraid and projecting what happened in my past on you. That wasn't fair."

He nodded and held her green-eyed gaze. "I know. And I'm not going to be obsessed with work. I can do both. Find the balance. Put you first. I want to put you first and Myles too. I want a house full of Thomas the Train toys and choo-choo background noise. I want to hear more baby cries and I want to make a life with you. I want to help you with the catering business and, dog gone it, Sadie, I'm even willing to back off the basil debate if you'll agree to marry me—at some point as I don't even have a ring. Yet."

She chuckled. "I kind of like our basil disagreements."

"Oh," he said as he kissed her lips, "I think we can find all kinds of things to disagree about."

Placing the coffee cup on the table, she embraced his waist. "So long as you know I'll always win."

He kissed her then. Intimately. Devotedly. A kiss that promised hope for a future and his wholehearted commitment to her and to Myles and their future family. "I think I'm the winner, and later today, I'd like to bring that swing set here for Myles. We'll figure out where you're going to stay temporarily. And by that, I mean—a very short basis."

Rocco didn't want to wait to marry Sadie. He'd do it today if she agreed.

"I like that plan. I like it a lot." A spark of the mischief he so loved about her sprang into her eyes. "Even more than your fettuccini."

"Blasphemy," he teased and her smart remark was cut off by his kiss.

He had a feeling he'd be cutting off her sass with kisses for a very long time to come.

And he was all in.

\* \* \* \* \*

*If you enjoyed this story, don't miss* Tracing a Killer,
*the next book in the Mountain Country K-9 Unit series!*

Baby Protection Mission
*by Laura Scott, April 2024*

Her Duty Bound Defender
*by Sharee Stover, May 2024*

Chasing Justice
*by Valerie Hansen, June 2024*

Crime Scene Secrets
*by Maggie K. Black, July 2024*

Montana Abduction Rescue
*by Jodie Bailey, August 2024*

Trail of Threats
*by Jessica R. Patch, September 2024*

Tracing a Killer
*by Sharon Dunn, October 2024*

Search and Detect
*by Terri Reed, November 2024*

Christmas K-9 Guardians
*by Lenora Worth and Katy Lee, December 2024*

*Available only from Love Inspired Suspense.*
*Discover more at LoveInspired.com*

Dear Reader,

I hope you enjoyed this story! Sadie deals with a lot of big feelings that many of us have over the course of our lives when disappointment, pain, grief and loss break us inside. But God is faithful, in all of it, even when it feels like He's ripping everything from us. We have to learn to trust Him. To know that He will bring beauty for ashes.

Please join my Patched In community and receive monthly newsletters. Sign up at my website at: www.jessicarpatch.com

Warmly,
*Jessica*

   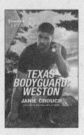